I0671971

PINE GROVE MYSTERIES

VOLUME 1

DAISY LANDISH

Editing by Rachael Lammie
Cover by Daisy Landish

BEACHES AND TRAILS
PUBLISHING

The Missing Mayor

A PINE GROVE MYSTERY

DAISY LANDISH

CHAPTER
ONE

SATURDAY, *Skies over the Northeast*

Green faded to orange then to lush red below as the twin-engine Cessna continued north. The Hudson River that emptied into New York Harbor meandered along six thousand feet below. As Peter flew over the Catskills and Finger Lakes, he sighed with contentment at the magnificent view of the northeast.

Peter hadn't realized how much he had missed it: the weather, the people, and the foliage. He missed the sun's angle in the fall as it hung south and kissed the gentle terrain that brought a soft, pine-scented breeze.

Having grown up just south of Boston decades ago, he now returned for good. He looked forward to taking possession of his family estate. Things seemed to have come full circle, now that his kids were working in New York and his divorce from Melanie was finalized.

The cool air of mid-autumn at this altitude gave Peter a clear view of the landscape far into the horizon. He felt a sense of peace descend upon him from behind the yoke as he returned to his northeast slice of heaven. The airspeed indicator was clocking 190 knots, but Peter couldn't tell as he looked out the window. All was still and picture-perfect.

His usual route would have taken him over Long Island. But severe weather had Peter riding the autumn storm's tails and enjoying the clear skies while flying inland over scenic Pennsylvania.

"The fifties will do that to you," he hummed along with the quiet radio. The empty co-pilot's seat presented no disagreement with anything he had to say. A short decade ago, Rina, his daughter, had occupied the front seat. She had learned to fly soon after her sixteenth birthday and was effectively his co-pilot. Matt, his son, and Melanie had always been happy to ride in the rear. Matt usually fell asleep, while Melanie read for most of the journey, regardless of where they went.

Now, and for the rest of his flying days, it seemed to be a certainty that it was just going to be him. Alone.

Peter didn't feel bad about any of it. He was as pragmatic as he was clear-headed. Life to him was like a river. You never see the same bend twice, he'd often say.

Peter had lived a semi-charmed life. After graduating Georgetown Law school, he'd landed a job with the FBI. He worked his way up to the Bureau's Council Office as one of the lead lawyers. Nothing exciting had ever happened in his twenty-five years at the Bureau, just tons of paperwork and court appearances. Odd how he'd never minded this until recently when the fact that his life had been at a standstill for years had begun to chafe.

I've needed a change for a while now.

His mind kept swinging between thoughts of his biological family and his work family. Each mile he clocked on his Garmin GPS took him a mile further from the former and a mile closer to the latter.

It felt good.

⁕

THE PORCH SWING creaked in the gentle autumn breeze forming a symphony with the leaves skittering across the walk with a dry rustling sound as they swirled in front of the house. "There's a lot to do," Peter murmured to himself as he walked through the front door.

A year's worth of dust greeted him. Canvas tarps lay on the furniture and cobwebs hung from the ceiling.

Mixed sensations coursed through him while competing memories vied for his attention. He chose not to entertain any of them for now, lest it tarnish his return.

There will be plenty of time for reflection later.

The landing beyond the main entrance split into cardinal directions with a chandelier hanging above the intersection. It was an heirloom, one that Peter had walked under every day as a kid, as did his father. It had started its life as an oil burner and was converted to electricity by his grandfather. Not fancy, by any stretch of the word, but solid and stoic. "Like Dad," Peter whispered as he looked up.

The solid floorboards returned a muffled sound as he stepped on them. Footprints followed him as he made his way across the dusty floor to the center where a large round table stood draped in white. Laying his keys on the table, his eyes followed the circular staircase that ascended to the upper floor. He followed his neck's momentum, turning his head to survey the north side of the house. Two large barn doors hung from the rails preventing his sight from entering the great hall. But memory filled in the gaps. Behind those doors was where he spent Saturday mornings watching cartoons.

Making his way past the dining room and into the kitchen, visions of his mother baking or preparing breakfast filled his mind. He could almost smell the cinnamon in the apple pie that would sit cooling by the open window. Memory guided him to the electrical room, where he checked the switches and reinstalled the fuses before pulling on the power lever.

Peter enjoyed bringing the old house back to life. Heat and water were next. As he ascended the stairs from the basement, he could hear the old boiler kick on and rumble as the air began racing through the conduits and out the vents.

He'd come prepared. He had a decent supply of canned food and bottled water amongst his belongings. He sat down to his first dinner of cucumber sandwiches and canned stew. He knew exactly what his mother would say. He could hear her now.

"That's all you're going to have for dinner, Peetey?"

He chuckled. When he was a kid, food was a family affair. And between the apple pies, barbecues, and steaks, 'skinny' was never a term used to describe young Peter. But things have changed.

The dust covers on his old bed had done an excellent job of preserving the mattress beneath it. The linen he found in the sealed closet looked as fresh as if it had been placed there that very morning. It was probably the last thing that his mother had done almost a year ago before she passed. Peter's bedroom linen had been washed religiously every fortnight since he graduated college, even if no one had slept in it.

Making his bed, he was grateful for his mother's meticulous housekeeping. He missed her hand in all things around the house. Peter fell asleep with mixed emotions. Happy that his mother's touch reached out through the linen that he slept on, but sad that there weren't many of those left. Eventually, he'd have to wash all of them, and that would be the end of the last things she touched.

He fell asleep thinking of his mother.

CHAPTER
TWO

SATURDAY MORNING, *Little Italy, Boston*

"Boss says we have a new job," Marconi began. Short and heavy around the waist, Marconi had been a captain since the nineties. He ran a crew that was into everything, from running numbers to supplying counterfeit goods, and even laundering dirty money. They even took on hit jobs and kidnapping targets from time to time.

"Yeah? When?" Russo asked. He was the skinnier of the two. Russo was young and full of ambition. He would do anything if he thought it would put him in his Boss' good books. It didn't matter what the job was; he was up for it.

"Tonight. He's already planned the whole thing out."

"What's the job, Marconi?"

"It's an easy peasy one. Just be back here at midnight. Bring those brothers, Vitto and Tommy, with you. No questions on this one. Just do as you are told when the time comes, and it will go down okay."

"Really, that's the way it's gonna be? Full of secrets?" Russo asked. He did not like being left in the dark. Discomfort descended upon the younger of the two mafia henchmen. "Alright, I'll see you back here at midnight." He grabbed his leather jacket and strutted across the private area of the pastry shop, which was a front for Marconi's operations. He made sure to slam the door on his way out.

SATURDAY, just before Midnight, Little Italy

Marconi sat at the back counter, his espresso sitting untouched. The job he was about to lead did not sit comfortably with him either. He had never been on the front-end crew. It was always all or nothing. Now, his Boss wanted him to pull off a job riddled with questions. That was enough to make the hair on his fat neck stand on end.

At midnight, a car pulled up and three doors slammed, one after the other. It didn't take long for two heavy-set men and Russo to come through the doors.

"Hey Marconi," Vitto said. "We are ready to go. SUVs all gassed up."

"Where did you get the vehicle from?"

"Out by Cambridge. In one of those long-term parking places," Vitto replied.

Marconi looked down at his empty cup. "Nice to see you thinking for a change. Last time someone reported the car you took as stolen before you even got out of town. I'll give you a bonus if you can ditch it before anyone calls it in."

Vitto winced at the sarcasm. Granted, the last job had been something of a mess. But since no one had gotten caught, he counted it as a success, of sorts.

"Where are we going, Marconi?" Tommy asked, with a quick glance at his partner, knowing Vitto was seething.

"He won't tell us," Russo said, his tone surly. "It's all hush-hush."

Tommy gave him a look. "So how do we play this?"

"Everybody, leave your phones on the table. Leave them on," Marconi said. When the three men had placed their phones on the table, Marconi handed them each a burner phone. "Don't turn this on until I tell you. Is that clear? I don't want the signal triangulating back to this place. You turn it on when I tell you, and *only* when I tell you. You got it?"

"Sure thing, Boss," the brothers replied while Russo just nodded.

New leather gloves, skull caps, and leather jackets awaited them. Each of them already had their bodysuits on. It was the standard operating procedure for Marconi's crew. If the authorities searched the vehicle, there would be no hair, fibers, or epithelial evidence that would lead them back to the crew members.

"Let's go. I give you details in the car," Macaroni replied.

The motley crew of gangsters trudged out the door and into the stolen SUV. No one said a word as they mentally prepared themselves for the night ahead, still not knowing what to expect.

CHAPTER
THREE

THE ALARM, set for five, hadn't rung yet, but Peter was already up due to the cold. Fall temperatures flirted with subzero numbers at night in these parts.

Removing his blanket was uncomfortable, but he had no choice.

"The heater must have fritzed," he muttered as he felt under the bed for his slippers.

He stumbled to the light switch and flipped it up and down a couple of times. Nothing turned on. With no light and no heat, Peter conscripted his blanket to be his guardian against the cold. Stars illuminated the clear night sky. The wind continued to sweep across the rolling terrain and through the woods, whistling its greeting and sending goosebumps through Peter's hair at the nape of his neck.

"I had forgotten how creepy silence can be," he said to himself. He was used to sirens and honking vehicles. Though to be fair, after three decades in the nation's capital, he hardly noticed the sounds of traffic anymore. Here in the country, the silence was deafening.

Standing at the window, Peter stared outside, facing north.

Barking in the distance suddenly caught his attention. It couldn't be a neighbor's dog as the closest house was at least ten miles away. *A stray?* Peter stared into the night to see if he could locate what was causing the dog's incessant barking. Then, he caught a glimpse of lights moving along the perimeter of his property.

Why would anyone be lurking around his property this time of night?

The car stopped. Another set of lights flickered.

Shadows seemed to move, but Peter couldn't distinguish them clearly. The first car made a three-point turn and went back the way it came. Another vehicle, that had been there waiting apparently, started up and left a few minutes later.

Car trouble? Not likely this far out. The property had been empty for a while. It was a prime target for those looking for a place to hide out, or worse, cook meth. While he hadn't seen any signs of trouble at the house, he hadn't had a chance to look around all that much. He really hoped that nobody was up to something nefarious so close to his property.

He found his phone for light, changed quickly, and hurried outside. Once he was sure which direction he'd seen the cars go, he headed cross country at a fast-paced jog. He started to run as he realized that whatever evidence he might hope to find could vanish quickly on a night like this, blown away by the incessant wind.

Instinctively, Peter moved faster toward the location he saw the two cars meet. At first glance, there was no indication that anything terrible had happened. But years of lawyering had taught him that when things seemed out of the ordinary, something sinister was likely afoot.

As he crossed the grassy knoll and approached the tree line, tall pines blocked the light of the stars. Peter slowed down to mind his footing. One wrong move and he could tumble down the side of the hill, breaking his ankle in the process. He moved slowly, not wanting to alert anyone else that might still be in the forest. He activated the night vision app on his iPhone to help him see where he was going.

The old path remained. He'd been seventeen the last time he was here, but he still remembered.

Stopping by a steep drop in the landscape, he heard the same bark. It was a lot closer now. The features of the terrain made it impossible to discern the direction of its origin as Peter turned to get a better sense of where it came from. Something about the bark told Peter that all was not well. The location where the cars had met was on the other side of the drop.

"Where are you?" Peter whispered, wondering if the dog might pop up in front of him, or worse, jump him from behind. Nothing in that bark sounded friendly.

As he crossed the stream and ascended the ridge, the barking stopped. Listening to nothing but the trees, Peter waited, hoping that another bark would give him a clue to where the dog was. But still nothing. In the end, he decided he couldn't worry about the dog right now. He had to get to where the cars had met.

Resuming his run, Peter kept his ear out for the dog that might be in trouble and continued up the slope. The air had gotten chillier, and the forest smelled muskier. Even the wind died down and left Peter to fend for himself with the shadows.

The barking returned, louder this time. It echoed off the valley walls. The sound seemed to come from everywhere.

Peter continued to move with as much speed as he could, keeping an eye on the night vision view on his phone's screen. He reached the cars' location at the top of the ridge. Turning back, he could see the hill where his house stood. It looked ghostly and deserted in the shadows. No one would have thought anyone lived there.

Peter looked around. He could see where the car had been parked on the gravel path. Depressions in the gravel indicated tire marks and scattered cigarette butts still casting up short tendrils of smoke corresponded with where the four car windows would have been.

Just then, something disturbed the gravel nearby. Peter turned rapidly from one direction to the next, looking for the origin of the barking, but couldn't tell. The sound moved closer and was quickening. A cold sweat broke along Peter's skin. He continued to search the shadows with his phone until he zeroed in on the shadows on the east side of the slope where it was darkest. Pointing his phone, he struggled to see what the night vision app would reveal. The barks had turned to growls, magnified by the terrain and Peter's imagination.

The animal burst out of the shadows and charged. Peter stepped back but knew not to run. You should never run when faced with a wild animal. You need to stand your ground. Otherwise, it will chase you and outrun you, without a doubt.

With teeth gnashing and fangs showing, the canine approached but drew back cautiously when it saw him. Peter turned on his phone light and the sudden illumination caused the dog to retreat. Every feature of the dog told a sad story.

The dog that was fully animated just moments ago now seemed calm and looked more tired than angry.

"Are you the one I heard last night?" Peter asked softly. The barking and growling tapered off as it sensed no threat from Peter. But uncertainty still ruled its demeanor.

"Where are you from, boy?" Peter asked, softening further and lowering his register, hoping his tone was soothing and coaxing.

"Woof," came a typical canine reply, as though responding to the question being asked.

"I mean you no harm." Peter turned his palm over and offered his fingers from a distance.

The dog instinctively approached, sniffing the air around him. Peter moved closer, stopping twice when the dog released a hesitant bark.

"Don't worry, I'm not going to harm you," Peter murmured, holding steady as he waited for the animal to accept him.

His cold nose finally reached Peter's warm hand, and Peter could hear a mild whimper as condensation snorted out of its nose, like a dragon breathing fire. Except this was no dragon. For all the fangs and teeth initially put on in the fierce display, the muddy lab was a gentle soul. Fear and hunger had driven him to caution.

"Atta boy. I'm not going to hurt you." Giving pets with one hand, Peter slipped the other into his hoodie's kangaroo pocket and retrieved a snack bar. One was usually there as a boost if he ran too far. He offered it to the dog, who was, by this point, completely focused on the wrapper, hoping what was inside was for him. Peter unwrapped the bar and gave it to him. "You like that, don't you boy?"

The dog was too busy eating to reply.

"I'm Peter. What's your name?"

"Woof."

"You understand me, do you?" Peter smiled at the possibility the dog was fully capable of communicating. "You look hungry. Want some more?"

"Woof."

"That sounds like a yes. So come on. Let's get you back to the house and get you a warm meal," Peter said.

Peter surveyed the place one last time before turning to leave. The cigarette butts suggested four men since none of the butts had lipstick stains on them. And all of them were the non-filtered kind.

The dog sat on the grass just off the path. Peter continued to look for clues as to why someone would be meeting out in the woods. As he turned to go, a glimmer in the gravel caught Peter's attention. The dog watched with interest as Peter bent to pick it up. It was a gold bracelet.

Peter held the bracelet up and inspected it with his phone light. It seemed shiny and showed no obvious signs of wear. More importantly, it clearly hadn't been in the dust for long. In this wind, which set up mini dust devils along the shoulder of the road and sent leaves and other debris across the pavement, this could only mean one thing.

Someone had left this here tonight.

CHAPTER
FOUR

JUST OUTSIDE BOSTON, *Dawn Sunday*

The stolen car with Marconi and his crew took its time moving north. The last thing they wanted was to attract any police attention by speeding on the highway.

"Tell them we're coming," Marconi commanded.

Russo nodded, picked up his burner phone and dialed. The man on the other end picked up in two rings.

"We're on our way. Should be there in about ten minutes," Russo said, his voice as cold as steel.

Russo listened a moment and hung up. "They're ready."

"Swing by the river, Tommy," Marconi said. "We're gonna ditch the burners in the river. Make sure you clean them for prints first.

"You know who she was, right?" Russo said.

"Quiet, Russo. You talk too much," Marconi yelled.

"I'm just sayin' that was a public official."

"What do you mean? What public official?" Tommy asked as he continued toward the river.

Russo nodded and fiddled with his lighter. "I've seen her on TV. She's making a lot of waves. Ambitious and feisty, that one."

Marconi turned around, sweating like he had a fever. "Shut it, Russo. I am warning you. That's enough out of you."

"You know as much as I do that the whole thing stinks," Russo replied.

"Yeah, Boss, this one stinks," Vitto chimed in. "I don't know who that lady was, but I know the driver in the other car. He's a paisan, but he works for the Cofta crew outta Brooklyn. What's his name, Vinnie I think."

The Cofta were the hard faction of the Russian mob. They were hard-core criminals that saw money laundering and gambling as child's play.

The new piece of information was enough to get Russo started again. "Now, would the Boss ask us to deal with a rival gang on this job?"

"Maybe...?" Vitto started, not realizing the question was rhetorical.

Russo snorted. "Okay smart guy, answer this. Why are *we* the front of it? Never mind, I'll answer for you. So, if anyone digs deep, who are they gonna find? Us. That's who. They gonna find us."

"Hey, Russo. Who was the broad?" Vitto asked.

Russo turned to the Boss, who refused to look any of them in the eyes.

"That was the Mayor of Pine Grove, Mayor Claire something," Russo replied.

"Claire Whitestone," Marconi chimed in a voice quieter than before. Everyone in the car knew that he was more worried about what had just gone down than they were. It explained all the precautions they seemed to be taking.

"So, wait, wait, wait, wait," Tommy jumped into the conversation, clearly rattled. "You're telling me we just kidnapped the Mayor of some dinky town? If this all goes south, we're the ones on the hook for it. Nah, nah, Marconi. This won't do at all."

"That's why we gotta be careful. This car gets lost, the phones get tossed, and no one's the wiser. No one would have seen us in the woods by the old Myers' place."

"Why'd you choose that place, Boss?"

"No one lives there anymore. The Myers kid lives in D.C. The old man and his wife died a year ago, so that entire place is deserted."

"How do you know so much about some old man in the middle of nowhere?"

Marconi thought about how he was going to answer. He decided that his crew could be trusted. "Old man Myers was a lawyer for the family," he said. "He was gunned down by the Cofta. No one outside the family knows about it."

"The Cofta – who that paisan in the other car now works for?" Russo asked, grimacing at the number of coincidences that were at play together.

Marconi shook his head, thinking the same thing as they pulled into the construction site for a new office tower near Copley Square. Lately, crews seemed to be working night and day, laying the foundation. By morning, the stolen car they were in would be beneath ten tons of foundation with no one the wiser.

CHAPTER
FIVE

DR. JESSICA STERN, the sign said. The name did not ring a bell as Peter eyed the humble exterior of Pine Grove's sole veterinarian's office. The office sat in the middle of town and shared Main Street with just a half dozen other small businesses. That's all that downtown Pine Grove was to the untrained eye: a stretch of red stone and two-story buildings, with the town hall on one end and the high school on the other. Both locals and visitors considered Pine Grove to be the perfect town, insulated from the hustle and bustle of a large city, yet a stone's throw from it. The best of both worlds, Pine Grove looked and felt like a southern town of the fifties. It was a great place to grow up or retire.

"Hi," Peter said as he pushed through the double glass doors and was immediately faced with a lady in a lab coat at the front desk. "Is the doctor in?"

"I'm the doctor," she replied, smiling. "We're too small to have a receptionist, so I pull double duty."

He should have known better. In a town as small as Pine Grove, all the businesses were owner-operated.

"Dr. Stern?" he asked, looking at the middle-aged face that was anything but stern. Kind and happy were the best ways he could describe her. Her face was softly rounded, and her smile welcoming.

"Jessica," she said to break the formality. "And who is this little fella?"

"A stray that I found in the woods this morning-"

"Woof," the dog interrupted.

"Hush," Peter whispered, as though he was talking to an old friend. "This doctor is going to help me fix you up. Be nice."

"Woof," the dog barked again, with no apparent intention of obeying.

Jessica laughed. "That's alright. I rather prefer the odd bark or two. Most dogs try to run back out once they realize they're at the vet."

"I bet."

"You were saying," Jessica said, redirecting the conversation.

"Oh, yeah. I found him this morning as I was jogging around my place." Peter figured she didn't need to know the cloak and dagger details of the morning.

"Oh, the poor thing," she reached for the dog, cradling him against her, laughing when the dog tried to lick her face. "I do have another patient coming in soon, but if you like you can leave him here. I'll check him over right after. Or were you wanting to surrender him...?"

He blinked at her. It had never crossed his mind to not keep the dog. "Well, I kind of thought he would want to stay with me..."

If anything, her smile grew wider. "In that case, I'll give you our new pet adoption special. The first vaccination is free."

"Thanks, Dr. Stern-"

"Jessica," she interrupted, scratching the dog behind the ears until his tail wagged madly.

"Sorry. Jessica. Thank you. I need to run some errands around town. Would two hours be okay?"

"Sure. Just fill out these forms and come back later. I will have him ready. What's his name?"

"I think he looks like Sam. What do you think? You know, like from *Lord of the Rings*?"

"Yeah. He definitely looks like a Sam." Jessica put a collar around him as Peter left for his errands.

To his surprise, the usually quiet town was aflutter. Cars zoomed past, police vehicles barricaded town hall, and people rushed through the streets. Reporters crowded the press area that had been set up across from the police station.

It looked like a campaign event. He shook his head and moved on, not really all that interested in local politics.

Peabody's had been in town for as long as he could remember. It had a grocer in the front, a hair salon at the side, and a laundry place in the back. There was also a hardware store on the premises. It had been that way ever since Peter was a kid. The only difference now was that Old Man Peabody no longer ran it. His daughter, Leah, did.

He crossed the newly-paved main drag, leaving the event at Town Hall half a block behind him. He headed for the door and pulled it, sending a chorus of bells ringing in the rear. A handful of people stood by the sole cashier's counter. A visibly much-older Leah ran items across a scanner for customers. The rest of the customers were all stopped in their tracks with their necks stretched upward, gazes aimed at the flat screen on the wall over the register.

Once more, Peter did not bother with the local gossip as he got what he needed. An hour passed, and his trolly, now overflowing with necessities for both human and canine, paved the way to the front counter that still buzzed with excitement.

When he got to the counter, Leah didn't spare a glance for him as her attention was still riveted on the screen.

Peter cleared his throat to get her attention. "Hi, Leah."

Leah turned. She had accumulated some weight, which was odd, Peter thought. Leah had been a cheerleader and one of the most popular girls in school. She never gave Peter the time of day, but she knew who he was since he did all her history assignments in the tenth grade.

"Do I know you?" she snapped. The smell of yesterday's bourbon and her last cigarette filled the space between them.

"It's Peter Myers."

That got her attention. "Peter? No, that's not you. It can't be. I haven't seen you since graduation. But no. It can't be you," she said with certainty, as she looked at him from head to toe, twice over.

"It's me," he said with a chuckle.

"Wow. You look good, Peter. You've lost so much weight!"

"Not that much." The boyhood crush he once had bubbled to the surface. But Leah was not the same person she was back then. A lot had changed. For a girl who was so into her own appearance in high school, she had long since lost her youth and good looks. Time had not been kind to her.

"I am sorry about your parents," she said, her tone softening, becoming kinder and gentler. "They were nice people. I saw Terry and Olivia at the funeral."

"Yeah. I wasn't able to make it," Peter said, suddenly faced with the ghost of his past decisions.

The shape of Leah's mouth suggested that her next question was related to why he didn't come back for the funeral. Peter had to stop it in its tracks before it saw the light of day. The only way to do that was to derail the conversation. "What's got everyone buzzing?" He nodded at the TV screen overhead.

"Oh, you don't know?! Mayor Whitestone didn't get home last night. Her husband, Henry Katz, reported it this morning."

"Didn't get home? What do you mean? She's missing??"

"Yeah, huh," Leah answered, sounding like an eighties high school kid again. "Rumor has it she might even be dead!"

CHAPTER
SIX

SUNDAY MORNING, *North Boston*

The Sunday morning crowd at one of Boston's most famous pastry shops was brisk. Over cannoli and coffee, patrons chatted with their friends while the establishment owner sat in the back with three of his men.

"They've finished pouring the concrete, Marconi," Russo said, between bites of his dessert.

"Think we need to stay low for a while?" Tommy suggested.

"God knows what they're gonna do to that mayor chick," Vitto replied. "I agree. We all should skip town for a while until things cool off. You know?"

"No. There will be no skipping and no running. We're not in grade school. Besides, that's not the real problem," Russo said.

Marconi, facing his plate of cannoli, raised his eyes. Seeing the look on Russo's face told him that the skinny man was afraid of the same thing he was.

"Cops are never the problem in this business. They're either too dumb to figure stuff out, or they're on the payroll," Marconi said.

The ominous tone of the conversation didn't sit well with the brothers. "What do you mean, Marconi?"

"It means that the Boss may be hanging us out to dry," Russo said.

Tommy and Vitto, now beginning to see the complete picture, slumped back in their chairs.

"We gotta play this cool. The Boss has never stabbed us in the back before, and I don't think he is doin' it now unless his arm has been twisted. He's giving us up to get himself out," Marconi suggested.

"I don't get it, Marconi," Tommy said.

"Yeah. Me neither," Vitto echoed.

"If someone is putting the Boss in a vice, then he puts us on the job because we're the best he has, then maybe he's hoping we cover our tracks, and no one gets hurt."

"No. I say we look after ourselves first. If the Boss is ratting us out, we better put this at his doorstep before *we* get into trouble."

"Shut up, Russo. You have a big mouth. You know that? No. Listen to me all yous—" They listened.

"We need to be smart. We can't go against the Boss. At least, not openly. I need the lot of you to swear on your families that this conversation never happened."

"Of course, Marconi. Our loyalty is to you first. It's always been that way," Russo assured him as the two brothers nodded emphatically.

Marconi went on to map out the plan. When he was done, Russo pledged to do his part, as did the two brothers. Marconi grabbed his leather jacket, drank the rest of his coffee, and moved out the back door without any of the patrons seeing him. A few minutes later, the brothers followed.

Marconi's plan was now in motion.

CHAPTER
SEVEN

LATE SUNDAY AFTERNOON, *Pine Grove*

"Alright, Sam. You stay here. The kitchen is all yours," Peter said, having bathed the dog and placed food in his new bowl. "I am going out for a while. You get some rest."

"Woof. Grrr," the dog replied.

"No. I mean it. No argument on this point. You need to eat and sleep. When you are all better, you can come with me then. End of discussion, young man."

Sam whimpered, suddenly realizing who was boss.

Peter donned his hoodie, pocketed his phone, and checked his laces before stepping onto the porch and looking around the property. It didn't take him long to run the path he'd taken in the darkness earlier.

He was used to crimes and underhanded dealings in larger cities, but this was Pine Grove. Why would there be sinister meetings in the dark? Why would the Mayor go missing? His mind turned over both puzzles. Not that it was any of his business. He should let the authorities handle that one.

Right?

When he arrived at the location, everything had been cleared. No tire marks, no cigarette butts.

Maybe not. If anything, this made him even more suspicious. If it had been kids joyriding or some other logical explanation, no one would have come back to remove cigarette butts or smooth out the gravel. This felt like the work of a pro.

I should have taken some pictures last night. Worked the scene.

Maybe the bracelet would provide more clues. He pulled it out and, using his phone's camera, activated the zoom mode. From what Peter could tell, it was 18-karat gold. The bracelet was thick but had refined workmanship. This was not something that was bought from a store window. It was made to order. It was definitely designed with a particular woman in mind. Charms in the shapes of trees, dolphins, rabbits, clouds, and an orb that looked like a representation of earth were inscribed all around the circumference of the bracelet. A broken clasp indicated there had probably been a struggle of some kind. The clasp was well-made, not something that would snap randomly. Someone would have had to pull on the bracelet to make it twist like that.

Had the wearer been a hostage, maybe?

He looked around some more to see if anything else presented itself. Then he remembered the second car. Peter walked up the road a few steps to see if he could find tracks or other evidence. He got lucky almost immediately. He found one cigarette butt, fresh, and not worn by the elements. Larger and filtered. It looked like it had been lit shortly before it was discarded. It was also a different brand from the rest. This time Peter took pictures of where it was lying before he picked up the cigarette and placed it carefully in a Ziplock bag he had brought with him. He used a pair of tweezers to keep from ruining any potential evidence. Thoughtful now, he gave the place one last look before starting his journey back to the house.

CHAPTER
EIGHT

SUNDAY EVENING, *North Boston*

The lunch crowd had taken some time to taper out, and it was not until four in the afternoon that the last of the customers left Marconi's Little Italy coffee shop. It was busier than usual with local neighborhood clientele and Bostonians from Cambridge in the east and Quincy in the south.

Marconi hung up the phone, having just spoken to the Boss. Everything seemed to have gone well, and he was given a bonus for pulling off the job. Neither man discussed why a rival gang was involved.

As Marconi parsed the conversation in his head, looking for messages and clues, Russo walked in, his face burdened with something. But what, Marconi could not yet tell.

"What's the matter?" Marconi asked as Russo sat down.

"There was someone there."

"Where?"

"At the Myers' place. I went there to clean up our tracks. And just after I got done, I heard footsteps. So, I hid in the bushes and see this fella, dressed in jogging clothes, come up and look around."

"Who's this fella? A cop?" Marconi asked.

"I don't know, but I took a picture of him."

"Let me see," Marconi said, his speech sped up, his voice an octave higher.

Russo retrieved his phone from his jacket and pulled up the photo of Peter in the woods.

"You're kidding," Marconi burst out. "This is the fella you saw. I can't be certain, but this looks like the Myers' kid. The youngest one. What's his name." Marconi snapped his fingers to jog his memory.

"You know this man?"

"Yeah, looks just like his father too at that age," Marconi replied. "Right. Peter Myers. He left home and was a lawyer like his old man but chose to work for the Feds."

Russo gasped. "This guy is a Fed? Then we got to get rid of him. He knows something. Why else was he looking around where we parked?"

"You telling me he saw something?" Marconi fumed.

"He must have. Otherwise, there would be no reason for him to come around. At least I already cleared all the stubs and dusted off the tire tracks. That's something. He might not know we were there."

"Did you manage to plant the evidence?"

"Yeah. Did as you said, Boss. Went down to Vinnie's hangout this morning. Just like you said, he was at the bar. Lifted one of the cigarettes he stuffed in the ashtray and threw it on the ground in the forest."

"Good. If anything comes of it, they'll use that one to trace it back to Vinnie. Serves him right for working with the Russians. I don't care if he gets life in the slammer."

"Myers picked up the cigarette, Boss."

Marconi did not like what he had just heard. He knew that Peter had zero tolerance for the mob or organized crime. For any crime, for that matter.

"You think he knows it was the mayor?"

"Oh, that's right. I forgot to tell you. He had a bracelet in his pocket that he picked up and looked at while he was looking around the scene," Russo told Marconi.

"Bracelet? *What* bracelet?"

"I don't know. I couldn't get a good look. It was a gold one with stuff hanging around it."

"Like the one the mayor was wearing last night?" Marconi asked, his voice elevated with urgency.

Russo thought for a minute. "Come to think about it, exactly like that," he answered.

Marconi slammed his fist down on the table. "How the *hell* did Peter get his hands on that?"

Russo frowned. "Looks like we got to take him out too, Boss."

Marconi was already shaking his head. "No. No one touches Peter. You understand? This family owes a debt of thanks to the father. His son cannot be touched. If anything, he is to be protected."

CHAPTER
NINE

MONDAY MORNING, MYERS' *Residence*

When Peter came down to the kitchen, it was just a little past 5 a.m. Sam greeted him with a wagging tail and an affectionate yelp. It had only been one day since they met, but already there seemed to be mutual respect between the two. Peter filled Sam's bowl with kibble and refreshed his water bowl.

A tall glass of water later, Peter began his stretches while Sam finished up his food. Then they both ran out the door. The run wasn't long as Peter didn't want to tire out Sam; the animal was underweight from being on his own and still on the road to recovery. The two were back in less than an hour.

Sitting on the porch, Peter stared out toward where the two cars had met two nights earlier. The local newspaper and the Boston Herald sat on his porch. He paid a lot to have it delivered, but it was worth it. Pulling the rubber band off, he opened the paper, thinking to himself how much he looked like his father right now. He didn't like the thought of that. He had respected his father, but he didn't want to be like him in the least.

Peter unfurled the Pine Grove Currant to see the front-page headlines: *Mayor Missing*. A picture of her occupied the left quarter of the broadsheet. She had undoubtedly aged since the last time he had seen her. Memories of her rushed back. She was the first woman he had fallen in love with. She was also the first woman who broke his heart. Trampled on it, in fact. And she was the person responsible for him and his father not being on speaking terms, something they were never able to reconcile before he died.

He stared at the picture and circumnavigated the torrent of memories that attempted to overcome him. Then, he noticed something peculiar. In the official photo as Mayor, she stood by her desk with her hands clasped in front of her. A bracelet dangled from her wrist. The same bracelet that was currently in Peter's pocket. The two crimes were connected. The missing Mayor and the intruders on his property were both parts of the same sequence of events.

"Let's go, Sam. Come on," Peter said as he ran into the house, grabbed his stuff, and ran out to the car. Pressing the start button shot the car to life, and Peter, not having any time to spare, jammed on the gas, spun his tires out of the gravel driveway, and headed into town.

Pulling into the parking lot across from the police station, he turned off the car.

"Stay here, Sam. You understand. Wait for me."

"Woof," Sam barked and promptly did the opposite.

Peter didn't have time to argue and chased after him. After a short romp about the town, Peter just barely caught him. Frustrated and not wanting to go all the way back to the car where he'd have to figure out how to get the dog to stay in while he shut the door, he finally just took the animal to the station with him.

"What can I do for you, Sir?" said the Sergeant at the main desk, regarding the dog at Peter's side with a raised eyebrow.

"My name is Peter Myers. I live out by Route 38 just outside town," Peter said.

"Yes, Sir, I know the place. What seems to be the problem?"

"Two nights ago, I saw two vehicles at the edge of my property. It seemed unusual for cars to be parked there, so I went to see what was going on. By the time I got there, they were gone. But I found this," Peter said, showing him the bracelet."

"Alright, Sir, I guess I can put it in lost and found, and if someone files a report—"

"No, Sergeant, this bracelet is the same as that one," Peter said, pointing to the picture of the Mayor hanging on the wall.

The Sergeant looked at one, then at the other until he came to the same conclusion. "Two nights ago, you say?"

"Yes."

"Hold on for a minute. I need to get the Captain in here. You'd better get comfortable in the meantime."

Peter was ushered into the conference room. A coffee machine sat in the corner where someone had just put on a fresh pot. There was also a box of doughnuts prepared for the new shift that would come in at the top of the hour.

While Sam sniffed at the table with the doughnuts, Peter walked around the table where the wall of information had been put up. The cops' primary suspect, it seemed, was Harlem.

Harlem was not a local. He was a loudmouth extremist politician. He didn't look like much. He was a rotund fellow with a pasty face and thinning hair. A recent poll of Pine Grove residents signaled that fifty percent of the town supported him. Peter couldn't see why. His reforms were drastic and would destroy the peace and serenity of the city.

Peter had to agree with Whitestone's platform, even if he had some personal issues with her. Mayor Whitestone promised to join green projects to combat the climate crisis and encourage larger corporations to shop in Pine Grove. Pine Grove could choose to either walk the path of smoke and pollution or the way of life and peace in the coming election.

"That's their primary suspect?" Peter said, frowning at the ineptitude he was witnessing. But he refrained from jumping to conclusions. They had shown him the courtesy of letting him walk into a room where they had all the formation on a current, active case. The right thing to do would be for him to play the role of a private citizen.

"Mr. Myers," a voice called out as the door opened.

"Yes?" Peter tugged on the leash, calling Sam back to him.

"And who is this fella, in my conference room, where there are no pets allowed?"

"I am sorry. I just couldn't get him to stay in the car," Peter said apologetically, mortified by the situation and almost forgetting why he was there.

The man who entered introduced himself as Captain Richard Donnelly. The Captain was a tall man, skinny, with thinning hair and a weary look around his eyes. Peter wondered if he'd slept since the Mayor went missing.

"I found a bracelet on my property after two cars had visited the place in the wee hours of the morning," Peter said, cutting right to the chase, not wanting to waste the man's time.

"What time do you say that was?" Donnelly asked, and the two men went over everything that Peter had seen and done in that time.

When Peter had got it all out, the Captain, who hadn't taken any notes, only nodded and smiled. "There are probably a hundred of those bracelets," he said. "It could have belonged to any number of women who had gone jogging there. We have our man. My boys will serve a warrant on him at daybreak, just in time for the Feds to arrive."

Peter shook his head. It was standard procedure for the Feds to get involved when it was a kidnapping case, especially one that involved a public official. The Federal Government was never lenient on kidnapping charges.

"How is Harlem your man?" Peter asked, incredulous at the steps that might have been taken to arrive at that conclusion.

"We got a tip, and it checks out." The Captain said, shifting uncomfortably in his chair, clearly not liking to be the one being questioned.

"You got a tip?" Peter asked with disbelief.

CHAPTER
TEN

MONDAY MORNING, *Pine Grove Police Department*

Captain Donnelly didn't even bother to take the bracelet into evidence. Peter was aghast at the shoddy police work that was underway. The Feds, according to Donnelly, would be there that morning. But by then, a potentially innocent man's reputation would have been dragged through the mud. That did not work for Peter. He figured there were two hours before the warrant would be served and another hour for the news to hit the wires.

Peter returned to his car with his canine buddy in the front passenger seat, and he thought for a moment.

A ding from his phone broke the silence that had descended on the car.

"Unknown number," Peter whispered as he looked at his phone. Tapping on it, he read the text message.

"Forget the Mayor's case. Don't look for trouble. From a friend," the message read.

Peter gasped. "What on earth?" The message was the break he was looking for. All this while he had no idea where to turn, but now, he had direction.

Scrolling through his contact list, he came across someone he hadn't spoken to in a couple of weeks. Tapping on it, he waited through several rings before the call was picked up.

"Peter?"

"Hey, Tiff, sorry to call you so early. I need a favor."

"What's new?" Tiff asked, clearing her morning voice. "How's Boston?"

"I don't know. I haven't gotten there yet. Still in Pine Grove."

Tiff and Peter were good friends. She'd helped him during his divorce.

"What do you need?"

"Listen. I know it's a little bit of a stiff ask, but I need you to do me a solid."

He heard her chuckle as she repeated the question she'd just asked. "What do you need?"

"Someone just messaged me. It's from a blocked number."

"You want to know who it is?"

"No. I am sure it's a burner. I need a little bit more than that. Think you can find out where the message originated from?"

"Wow. That's a bit of a stretch. But I'll take care of it. When do you need it?" Tif asked.

"As soon as possible, please."

"Alright, I'll call you back."

Peter hung up and looked at Sam. "Don't worry, Tiff will come through for us. Just give her a few minutes."

No sooner had he reassured Sam, his phone rang. It was Tiff.

He smiled. Right on cue. "That was quick. What did you get?"

"The last message that went to your phone came from a burner, alright. That burner is now pinging a cell tower in North Boston."

"Can you triangulate it for me and get me an address?" Peter asked.

"Sure. You want fries with that?"

Peter laughed.

"Hang on the line. I'll ping it now."

Less than ten seconds went by.

"The phone is currently on, and it's at a coffee shop slash pastry joint called Marconi's in North Boston. These thugs are too stupid to ditch a burner."

"Do you need a street address?"

"No. Unfortunately, I know where that is."

"Unfortunately?"

"I will explain that to you some other time. Just not now. Thanks a million, Tiff," Peter said and hung up as he put the car into gear and backed out of the parking lot in a hurry.

He glanced over at Sam who was looking with interest out the open window, as though wondering where they were going next. "We're off to Boston, Sam. Ever been to Boston?"

CHAPTER
ELEVEN

MONDAY MORNING, *Marconi's*

Russo sat across from Marconi as they planned out what to do next. Tommy and Vitto had done what they were told and followed Vinnie from afar, watching all the places he went. He finally ended up in a warehouse in Alston. Now Marconi had the whole picture. He had their conversation, which detailed the whole setup, captured on video.

"We have our insurance policy," Marconi told Russo.

"You know how to play this one, Boss. But I gotta tell you. I don't see how I can work for the old man anymore," Russo said, talking about the big Boss, Marconi's Boss.

"You can't say that, Russo. You have to bide your time. For now, we have all the evidence we need. You keep a copy of the audio and video, and I'll keep a copy. If anything happens, it's all here."

"Yes, Boss."

"You better get home, or else Louise is going to give me an ear full," Marconi said finally, not entirely satisfied with their plan, but knowing it was the best they could come up with under the circumstances.

Russo laughed. "No way, Boss. She loves you like a father. You can do no wrong in her eyes," Russo said as he got up and grabbed his coat. It had been a long night.

He walked to the door, opened it, and jumped back, startled. "Hey, Boss, look who's here," Russo said, standing at the door.

Marconi glanced up, his widening in surprise, and gestured for Russo to leave.

With Russo gone, Marconi reached up to Peter and gave him a hug. "It's been a long time, kid. A long time. I am sorry for your ma and pa."

Peter didn't say anything but nodded. Sam, however, began growling.

"Sam. Quiet," Peter commanded. This time Sam obeyed.

"Please, Peter. Have a seat."

"So, you sent me the message?" Peter asked.

Marconi nodded.

"Why are you involved? Or should I ask *how* are you involved?"

Marconi told him the whole story of how it was all a job, and he didn't know it was the Mayor until he had her. He didn't stop there though. Marconi went on to tell him that he knew where the Mayor was and told Peter about the video.

"So, Harlem has nothing to do with this?"

"Not that I know of."

"Who then?"

Marconi shook his head. "It's on the video. But I can't show it to you. It's my insurance policy, and there are some mighty people there that could do you and me a lot of damage."

"No, Marconi, you have to tell me. You have to show me."

"I can't. My Boss is on that video, and so is the head of the Cofta."

"Look, if I get your Boss, and I know the Feds are trying hard to get him, then you'll rise to his place. Yes?"

"Yes. Technically, I'm next in line."

"So, give me the evidence. I'll see to it that he is put behind bars."

"But this wasn't his idea. This isn't a mafia job."

Peter frowned. "Then who ordered the kidnapping, Marconi?"

"She did."

"She who?"

"The Mayor. It was all staged. Don't you see? She was running neck and neck with Harlem. She staged the kidnapping so that she would get the sympathy vote. She hired the Cofta to do the job."

"Why the Cofta?"

"Because her family, her father, and grandfather have always been connected to the Russian mob."

Peter's eyes widened. He sat back in his chair to think this over. "Did you know that she was the one who told me that my father worked for you guys?"

"When?" Marconi asked.

"Just after graduation."

"And that's why you stopped talking to him?"

"Yes. And to my mother for protecting him."

"That's why you didn't attend their funeral?"

Peter nodded.

Marconi was quiet while he considered his next move. It didn't take long. He'd already figured he was going to have to go this far back when he'd set certain things in motion. It didn't make the decision go down any easier though. "Alright. Here, I made a copy for you just in case I had a change of heart. Here. Take it. Go and do what you must. I just hope you don't lead them back to me."

Peter made no such promises. Instead, with Sam in pursuit, he rushed back to his car and drove to Federal Plaza. He knew the Assistant Director that headed the Boston Field office, so it wasn't hard to get in to see him. Thankfully, Peter was just in time. He was about to leave for Pine Grove.

Within a few hours, the whole case was wrapped up. The heads of the Cofta and Boston Mafia were arrested, as was the sitting Mayor of Pine Grove.

Peter and Sam headed home. Peter didn't know what awaited them, but hoped their adventures would include more scenic, and non-life-threatening, excursions through the beautiful countryside of his childhood home.

The End

Dead Man Dalton

A PINE GROVE MYSTERY

DAISY LANDISH

PROLOGUE

MR. DALTON SAT in his armchair, stroking the barrel of his shotgun. He hadn't loaded it yet, but knowing it was there gave him a sense of comfort.

The sound of the TV gently hummed as Mr. Dalton lowered it to almost mute. With the subtitles on, he didn't need the sound on. But he found he couldn't sit comfortably in his home in silence. Loneliness was a terrible thing, and he was afraid of what lurked in the shadows around his house.

The fireplace gently warmed the room, casting shadows of orange across the dirty, unkempt rug that hadn't been vacuumed in over a year. Then, finally, the soft crackle of the ember's lulled Mr. Dalton, and his eyes fluttered shut.

Suddenly, his eyes snapped open, and he could hear rustling in the bush at the back of his house, a sound he had become accustomed to – A sound he wished would go away. Someone was out there....again.

Mr. Dalton couldn't remember when it started, but he should have known it would. You can never outrun your past, no matter how hard you try. The guilt had eaten at him for years, and Mr. Dalton often wondered if this was karma, a payback he deserved.

Turning off the lamp on the side table next to his chair, he picked up the gun and slowly crept to the back door. Pushing the small fabric that covered the square glass window, he peeked outside, hands shaking, causing the gun to rattle. He had forgotten he hadn't loaded it; the shells sat next to the lamp in the other room.

This is my home. They will not make me run from my home! Mr. Dalton vowed.

Taking several deep breaths to calm his nerves, he pushed the door open with such force that it slammed against the outside wall, startling birds in the trees and causing them to take flight.

"Go away! Leave me alone! This is your final warning; do you hear me? Next time you will meet the business end of my shotgun! I will kill you; I promise you that!" Mr. Dalton yelled.

His words echoed into the night. Mr. Dalton stood waiting, listening. Searching the blackness of the woods surrounding his home, Mr. Dalton saw nothing, which was unsurprising since his eyesight wasn't what it used to be. Was that a shadow on the porch or a figment of his imagination?

A cold fall wind pushed through the trees, sending a shiver down the old man's spine. After waiting a little longer and finally satisfied he had scared away whoever stalked his home, Mr. Dalton stormed back inside, slamming the door, muttering to himself.

"Know what you did...I did....my house! It's my house! My Sylvia."

⁘

THE OLD MAN'S terrified voice rang through the trees. The simplest of acts was having the desired effect; Mr. Dalton seemed positively unhinged. Revenge was sweet. The old man would pay.

It appeared that Mr. Dalton might shoot for a second, but concern faded when his shaking hands rattled the empty gun.

The old fool must have forgotten to load it.

The plan was reaching its end, it wouldn't be long now. But first, a trap must be set. The old man must be seen as crazy; that way, it would look less suspicious.

The old man had made that part of the job easy. From the cover of the trees, lights could be seen flickering to life in the houses next door.

That's right old man, scream and shout. Let it all out. You are digging your own grave.

CHAPTER
ONE

OCTOBER, *New England*

The leaves from trees decorated the parking lot in shades of browns, oranges, and reds, giving a satisfying crunch underfoot. Peter Myers pushed his shopping cart around the store. Fall in New England was the perfect time for soups, casseroles, and other comfort foods. But sausage casserole wouldn't be sufficient for the meal he had planned. This was no ordinary meal; it was a first date with the beautiful, kind, always smiling Dr. Jessica, the vet.

For some reason, she had implanted herself in Peter's mind ever since she helped Peter out with Sam. And Sam swiftly gave him an excuse to see her again when he hurt his paw out on a morning run with Peter. So, the pair met again as if it were fate – or canine intervention – and Peter seized his chance to ask her out.

The date was set for the following evening, giving Peter enough time to calm his nerves and straighten the house. Jessica was coming around for dinner, so it had to be special. Grabbing a few steaks and extra for Sam, red wine, and a cheesecake, Peter walked to the checkout desk with a smile and a spring in his step.

"That everything?" Leah asked, not paying attention.

Even after a month's return, Peter still found how much Leah had changed. Whenever he went for groceries, it was clear that Leah wanted to be anywhere else but the store.

"That's everything. Thanks, Leah," Peter smiled, handing over the cash.

Leah grunted something that resembled acknowledgment and shrugged as she handed Peter his change and stuffed his shopping into brown paper bags. Peter bid Leah farewell and headed to his car, groceries in hand. With every step closer, his mind raced with thoughts of Jessica and the excitement of the evening to come.

Peter was not usually the type to listen to music in the car, but this was a special occasion. Fiddling with the radio to find the perfect station, Peter began to reverse out of his parking spot when he was suddenly and forcefully shot forward. His head tapped the staring wheel, dazing and confusing him momentarily.

Quickly checking himself over the rearview mirror, Peter was pleased to find he wasn't hurt, just a little surprised. He was sure he had been paying attention and hadn't seen anything coming when he reversed his vehicle. Then, startled by guilt and concern raging in the pit of his stomach, Peter jumped from his truck to find his old science teacher Mr. Dalton.

Mr. Dalton looked like he had seen better days. His hair had long since thinned and was white from old age. With unkempt hair and clothes that looked a little worse for wear, Mr. Dalton looked back at Peter, dazed and just as startled. Startlement turned to anger, and the old man's face turned red with rage.

"Look what you did! Look! My groceries are ruined! This is your fault! Why were you not watching where you were going?" Mr. Dalton screamed at Peter, wagging a finger as he strode closer.

Peter glanced at where the two cars had collided. Both bumpers were scratched and badly dented with smashed rear headlights. Yet, the only thing that concerned Mr. Dalton was his groceries. Looking at the back window, Peter could see why Mr. Dalton was angry. Eggs leaked from the carton, milk poured over the back seats, and a few other pieces lay askew.

"I'm so sorry, Mr. Dalton, I didn't see you when I reversed. You must have been in my blind spot. I will pay for the damage to the car, of course…." Peter began.

It was hard not to notice how, since a small gathering of on-lookers had appeared, Mr. Dalton had become visibly distressed. His hands shook, he fidgeted with the hem of his jacket, and his eyes darted around the crowd. Then, interrupting Peter's apology, Mr. Dalton began to scream again.

"I don't care about that! Just move your car. I want to go home! Now! Move!"

"Please allow me to replace your groceries before you go," Peter insisted.

"I said I don't care! I want to go home! Move your car before I get in it and move it for you!" Mr. Dalton roared, his face growing red and flustered.

An older lady with a yappy little dog, who hadn't stopped barking at Mr. Dalton since he began yelling, stepped forward. Scooping her frightened pooch into her arms like a child, she gently tapped Peter on the shoulder.

"Do you want me to call the police for you?" she asked.

"No! No! No! Just move! And get that dog to shut its trap!" Mr. Dalton yelled.

He seemed even more agitated since the police were mentioned. The old lady gasped and took several steps back, clinging to her canine companion for dear life.

Concerned but not wanting to push the old man further, Peter nodded and reluctantly moved his vehicle. Then, stepping out, Peter watched as Mr. Dalton continued to scan the crowd before jumping in and speeding off, almost running a red light as he tore down the street.

Turning back to the store, Peter saw Leah leaning against the wall outside, cigarette in hand, staring blankly into the distance.

"Hey, Leah. What's wrong with Mr. Dalton?" Peter asked.

She took one last drag and blew out a cloud of smoke, tossing her butt on the floor and crushing it with her boot. Leah shrugged before heading back inside.

CHAPTER
TWO

MYERS' *Residence*

Sitting in the backyard with Sam resting on his feet, Peter tried to read the paper for several minutes. But all he could think about was the events from earlier that day. Perhaps he had been distracted thinking about Jessica or tapping along with the radio for the accident to be partially his fault. He racked his mind and was sure he had checked his rearview, side mirrors, and blind spot before reversing.

But that wasn't the only thing that plagued Peter's mind. Mr. Dalton had looked shabbier than Peter had ever seen him. Peter thought back to when Mr. Dalton was his science teacher; he was always a man who took pride in his appearance and had expensive tastes regarding clothes, especially his shoes. Peter worried about poor old Mr. Dalton. How he shifted uneasily and panicked around the small crowd of on-lookers wasn't the strong-minded Mr. Dalton Peter remembered.

"Was it the crowd or the fact someone offered to call the police?" Peter asked.

"Woof," Sam barked softly to answer Peter's question.

"Yeah, Mr. Dalton might not have insurance. You are right, boy," Peter muttered, stroking Sam on the head.

If Mr. Dalton didn't have insurance and had let himself go a bit, perhaps he was in financial trouble. Guilt pooled in Peter's stomach. If the old man was having money issues, Peter had just ruined possibly a month worth of food that couldn't be replaced. Peter couldn't sit back and let a man he respected go hungry, not when he had the means to help.

"No, I can't sit back and do nothing," Peter said. Grabbing his coat, wallet, and keys, he headed back to the store.

With the help of Tiff, Peter's trusted agent friend; it didn't take long for Peter to have the correct address for his old science teacher. Pulling up to the street, Peter sighed. Unfortunately, not all the houses were numbered; it would be tricky to find exactly which house was the right one.

"What are you looking for, friend?" came a woman's voice from a house across the street. She was poking her head out of the window.

Peter swiftly deduced that this person, whoever she was, was the street's nosey neighbor. Every street had one, after all.

"I'm looking for Mr. Dalton's house," Peter replied, unpacking the groceries from the car.

"That one there, with the messy lawn," pointed the woman as she closed the blinds and headed back inside.

Turning, it was apparent which house she was referring to. All the other lawns were mowed to perfection, lush and green with a few sprinklings of autumn leaves. However, Mr. Dalton's yard was at least four feet high and dead, the paint on the outside of his house had long flaked off, and the redwood door was in disrepair.

Strolling up to the front door, Peter set the groceries down on the front porch, stood, and prepared to knock when crazed ramblings grew louder from the other side.

"Get off my property!" came Mr. Dalton's voice.

Suddenly the door flew open. Standing in the doorway was Mr. Dalton brandishing a shotgun.

"Get off my porch! Go away! Leave me alone!" Mr. Dalton yelled, waving the shotgun in Peter's direction.

Thinking fast, Peter took several steps back, raising his hands above his head. Heart pounding, Peter kept his eyes locked on the barrel of the gun.

CHAPTER
THREE

DALTON RESIDENCE

"Mr. Dalton, please, I only came to replace the groceries I damaged earlier on," Peter said, trying to calm the situation.

"I told you I didn't care about that! Don't you youngsters listen?"

Peter chuckled internally; it had been a few years since anyone referred to him as a youngster. But in comparison to Mr. Dalton, the old man wasn't entirely wrong. Mr. Dalton was close to eighty years old, at least. Time had aged his features, and age-related spots decorated his face.

"Mr. Dalton, please. Put the gun down," Peter said softly.

"It's my first amendment right to bear arms. I'm protecting myself; now go before I shoot. This is your final warning!" Mr. Dalton yelled cocking the gun with a telltale clink.

"All right, I'm leaving," Peter admitted defeat.

There was no talking sense into the old man. He was simply crotchety and mean, trodden on by life that had dampened his spirits. Not wanting to agitate the old man any further, Peter walked back slowly to his car, keeping a close eye on the shaking gun aimed directly at him. Getting into his car, Peter sighed deeply before slowly driving away.

PETER DIDN'T FULLY KNOW why, but even with the growing wind of October, he ended up sitting outside a café on the town's main strip. Of course, it made more sense to sit inside. But as Pine Grove had changed so much since he was last there, Peter decided to people-watch. Images raced through his thoughts. He thought about Leah, what she was like in high school and who she was now. Marconi crossed his mind and all the drama of the previous month. And finally, Mr. Dalton.

It saddened Peter to see his old teacher in such a way. Questions spun in his mind. Did Mr. Dalton have anyone to care for him? What had happened to make him so on edge? And more importantly, had he ever hurt anyone with that shotgun? Peter worried that with a weapon of such caliber and in his nervous state, Mr. Dalton might wind up hurting himself or someone else.

Peter remembered Mr. Dalton's science classes fondly. Mr. Dalton spoke of science with such passion that even the unruliest student was enthralled by his words. He took a potentially complicated and boring subject and made it fun. To his students, Mr. Dalton was a hero, a superhero. Mr. Dalton once commanded a room; people had stopped and listened. And now, the poor man seemed to cower at the world. It broke Peter's heart to see a man he always respected reduced to a fragment of the man he used to be.

His eyes followed the bustling crowd of people pulling their coats tighter around themselves, guarding against the wind. The leaves found new homes around town, scattering the streets as cars zoomed past. Peter's eyes fell on Leah coming out of the post office next door. He hadn't noticed her go in, and he had been sitting outside for so long that his coffee had gone cold.

"Hey Leah, do you have a minute?" Peter called, waving Leah over.

Shrugging, Leah joined him at the table.

"What's up? I'm a bit busy," Leah said.

"I won't keep you long, I promise. I was just curious, what's Mr. Dalton's story? Unfortunately, he isn't as I remember him."

Pulling a cigarette from her purse and lighting it, Leah took a long drag, blowing the smoke away from Peter, which drifted back his way with the wind. Then, shrugging, she tightened her scarf around her neck.

"I'm not sure of the full story, but he retired a few years ago. From what I remember, it was health issues, and there was a big stink about it, too," Leah answered.

"Stink? How so?"

"It wasn't his decision."

"He was forced to retire?" Peter asked for clarification.

Leah nodded, taking another long drag.

"Forget about him; he is a nutcase. Neighbors say they can hear him arguing with himself. And a few times, he has come out of his house waving that damn shotgun around. It wouldn't surprise me if he killed someone or himself," Leah said.

"I see," Peter said.

"I mean, everyone knows he has money, so why is he suddenly acting like he is poor? It is beyond me. As I said, nutcase," Leah said, finishing her cigarette, "Anyway, I got to go."

"One more thing, please. What was his health issue?"

"Some sort of mental breakdown, I think, I don't know," Leah shrugged, hooking her bag over her shoulder and leaving Peter with his thoughts.

Peter disagreed with Leah. Peter didn't believe Mr. Dalton was a nutcase. If anything, Leah's observations only drew more concern. Something didn't add up. There was a missing piece to the puzzle. An academic like Mr. Dalton wouldn't just shift overnight. And for someone who took his career as seriously as he did, for him to be forced to retire said something was wrong. From what Peter could remember, Mr. Dalton always hated guns, but now a shotgun appeared to be his companion.

Is Mr. Dalton afraid of something? Of course, the biggest unanswered question was why he was so scared.

CHAPTER
FOUR

MYERS' *Residence*

It was surprisingly calm for an October morning, with a slight chill in the air but nothing bad enough to put Peter off his morning jog.

"Come on, boy, time for some exercise," Peter said, holding the door open.

"Woof, Woof," Sam replied, charging off ahead.

Peter chuckled to himself, gently jogging after Sam through the woods surrounding the property. The weather wasn't cold enough to warrant frost, but Peter knew it would be a harsh winter from the crushing underfoot. New England was beautiful in the fall. Peter admired the scenery as he ran, taking in all the sights, sounds, and smells of fall. So gorgeous; no other word would suffice.

"Come on, boy, time to head home," Peter said, turning off the trail.

Peter had recently changed his morning jog route. He started through the trail at the back and headed around the neighborhood. He waved good morning to the few people awake at that time of day. Then, he finished his run at the front of his house.

"Woof!" Sam barked swiftly, following suit.

As Peter jogged up the gravel path outside his house, he saw a sight he wasn't expecting. Parked outside his house was a police car.

One officer sat inside, visibly scrolling on his form, while the other stood leaning against the vehicle.

Sam stopped, offering a low growl in warning.

"Shush, Sam, it's all right," Peter soothed.

"Morning officers, how can I help?" Peter asked, opening the door and letting Sam run inside.

"Peter Myers?" asked the officer leaning against the car.

"That's me," Peter answered.

"We need you to come to the police station," said the officer whose name stood proudly embroidered above his badge. Officer Samson.

"What is this regarding?" Peter asked.

"Mr. Dalton was found dead this morning, and our sources say you were the last person to see him alive," Officer Samson said, his fingers fiddling with the handcuffs on his hip.

It was hard for Peter not to let his eyes drift to the loosely veiled threat. Was he under arrest? Was he being asked to come in voluntarily, or had Sam picked up on a bad vibe Peter had missed?

"Am I under arrest, officer?" Peter asked.

Sam, sensing the growing tension, popped his head out the door. Standing guard, he let out a low growl, standing close to Peter's hip.

"Quiet, Sam," Peter said, gently stroking the dog's head.

"You are not under arrest. No, we want you to come with us to answer some questions. A neighbor's video cam puts you at the crime scene. I believe you are a lawyer, so you understand the law," Officer Samson replied, his eyes not leaving Sam, who still stood offering soft growls.

"I understand. Let me lock up, and I'll be right with you," Peter offered.

Reluctantly, Sam went inside, jumping at Peter as if trying to convince him to stay. Peter didn't like locking Sam up in the kitchen, even if it was spacious enough for him. Usually, Sam had free roam the house while he was out. But Peter could sense Sam's anxiety at the police presence and needed to keep him calm.

"Sorry, boy, but you will have to stay here. Drink, rest; I'll be back soon," Peter said, closing the kitchen door behind him.

Sam barked in protest; his claws scratching at the door could be heard throughout the house. Soft whimpers followed Peter as he walked to the front door, pulling at Peter's heartstrings. Peter waited at the front door for Sam to quiet before leaving and heading to the police station with the officers.

CHAPTER
FIVE

PINE GROVE POLICE *Station*

Walking through the police station, Peter walked with his head held high. He knew he was innocent and would not let the officers trying to intimidate him. Peter was a good lawyer and knew the law; he also knew evidence would prove him innocent.

Officer Samson directed him to a small interrogation room at the back of the station, no different from the rooms Peter had sat in before with his clients. He knew he would be left there for a while to stew, a poor effort to make him nervous. But Peter was calm, relaxed, and waiting. Sitting in the purposefully uncomfortable plastic chair, Peter sat with his hands clasped in front of him on the desk. The sound of the station was ringing through the door.

Finally, Officer Samson returned with the police captain. It was the captain Peter met during the mayor's case only a month ago. Peter got the same feeling then as he did now; something was off about the captain. Peter just didn't know what. But Peter knew if anyone could find out what that man was doing, it would be him, all in good time.

"So, Mr. Myers...."

"Peter, please," Peter interrupted.

Peter was not the type to interrupt people; he found it rude. But he wanted to let them know he wouldn't be intimidated at that moment.

"Of course….Peter. Where were you last night?" the captain asked.

"What time specifically?" Peter asked.

The captain exchanged a look with Officer Samson. Either they didn't have an accurate time of death, or they were not expecting Peter to ask his own questions.

"I'm asking the questions here, Mr. Myers. We have footage putting you at the crime scene," the captain said, opening a folder.

Inside sat a screenshot of Peter leaving Mr. Dalton's house. From what Peter could see, it was just before he drove off. He remembered it well.

"So I've been told," Peter said, his eyes flashing to Officer Samson.

"Why were you at the Dalton residence?" the captain asked.

"I had a run-in with Mr. Dalton earlier that day. We had a small crash in the parking lot at the grocery store. He seemed shaken up and complained that I had spoilt his groceries. I felt for him, so I went to deliver new ones. The footage you have will show me dropping them off. When I arrived, he made it clear he didn't want me there, so I left," Peter said, folding his arms across his chest.

"Yes, we have footage of you leaving," Officer Samson said.

"So, officers, tell me. If you have footage of me leaving, why am I here? The footage will show that I left swiftly after I arrived."

The officers exchanged a look once more before Officer Samson, who seemed less intimidating than earlier that morning, continued.

"A neighbor called in the incident. They were leaving for work when they saw Mr. Dalton's door ajar. When they went in to investigate, they found him dead. Looks like blunt force trauma to the head. His skull was in pieces on the floor. When we arrived, they offered up their doorbell footage as evidence."

"So….what happened to the footage from the rest of the day? Because I arrived at Mr. Dalton's house just after one o'clock in the afternoon and left all of five minutes later with Mr. Dalton very much alive, waving a shotgun in my direction," Peter said.

"Yes, we are aware of Mr. Dalton and his gun," Samson offered.

"Officer Samson, will you examine the footage at the time Mr. Myers mentioned? Then, I shall continue the interview," Donnelly said.

Peter sat button-lipped, watching Officer Samson leave. Officer

Donnelly seemed visibly annoyed when Officer Samson gave Peter details of the case. Perhaps getting rid of him was the officer's way of keeping information from Peter.

"Look, officer...."

"Captain, actually," Donnelly gave a sly smile.

Peter fought not to roll his eyes, offering a soft smile.

"Apologies....Captain Donnelly, I had nothing to do with this. I brought Mr. Dalton groceries and nothing more. I assure you that the time of death will clear up my involvement. Do you have any more questions for me, or am I free to leave?" Peter asked.

The captain glared at Peter silently before closing the folder and tucking it under his arm.

"You are free to go....for now. We will wait on the results of the autopsy. But do not leave town, or I will arrest you for perverting the course of justice," the captain said while he stood.

"I wouldn't dream of it, officer....sorry, captain," Peter said.

As Peter headed home, his mind went into overdrive. The captain hadn't offered any information about how exactly Mr. Dalton had passed, what time, or even asked many questions. Was he expecting a confession there and then? Purely based on some grainy doorbell footage? What was the captain up to? Was he trying to use Peter as a scapegoat? Either way, Peter knew from the investigation with the mayor that the captain's police work was not up to scratch. If Peter wanted answers, he would have to find them himself.

CHAPTER
SIX

HIS FRUSTRATION GREW; Peter didn't like being kept in the dark. Too many questions were left unanswered. If the police had footage of Peter leaving, where was the footage? Why had they not considered that he wasn't covered in blood? Peter had seen enough crime scene photos over the years to know a thing or two about blood splatter in a case like this.

I think it's time to do a little investigation of my own, Peter thought, heading home to collect his car and to see Mr. Dalton's nosey neighbors. Arriving at Mr. Dalton's street, Peter pulled up and scanned the houses across the street for a video doorbell. Three had them, but with a familiar face poking out of the window, it was easy for Peter to deduce which house the footage had come from. The name on the letter box said *Logan,* and from what Peter had seen at the station, which meant the Taylor who had handed in the footage was a woman. Peter remembered seeing the witness' name on the folder before the police captain pulled it away. Another instance of the police chief's sloppy police work – Never let a murder suspect know any details about potential eyewitnesses.

Locking eyes with Peter, the woman who directed him to Mr. Dalton's house only the day before swiftly closed the curtains and rushed inside. It appeared she was the type to be in everyone's business. Peter strode to the door and pressed the large blue circular light on the doorbell. He waited patiently for a moment before a woman opened the door.

"Hello, Taylor Logan, is it? I'm Peter. I was wondering if I could borrow a moment of your time to ask about Mr. Dalton?" Peter smiled softly.

"I know who you are. If you don't leave, I'm calling the police," she insisted.

Peter looked Taylor over for a woman just sitting at home staring out and spying on the neighbors. She was dressed as if she was about to go out for drinks with the girls. The telltale red bottoms of her shoes that lay on the floor in the hall beside her bare feet screamed Louboutin. Her dress and jacket were clearly designer too. She held herself with a level of self-confidence and arrogance, folding her arms across her chest and resting her shoulder against the door frame. A smug look of superiority spread across her face.

"How do you know who I am if you only saw my car?" Peter challenged.

Taylor looked back at Peter, visibly startled with wide eyes. His statement made it clear that he had seen the footage she handed to the police, and she wasn't expecting to be interrogated, not at her doorstep. Peter waited for a response, silently letting Taylor know he wasn't going anywhere without answers.

"I saw you with my own eyes," she muttered, her eyes falling to the ground.

"I mean no harm, Mrs. Logan. I only want to ask a few questions; then I will leave you to your day," Peter said.

"I don't have to answer your questions! I know what you did! Now go away!" Mrs. Logan snapped, her voice raising in volume.

"Who is that at the door?" growled a croaky dry voice from inside the house.

Loud pounding footsteps echoed through the hall behind the door.

"Who is making all that noise?"

Suddenly, the door swung open. Peter was face-to-face with his old school buddy, Greg Logan. Peter couldn't believe he hadn't recognized the name sooner. How could he forget Greg Logan? Greg was once the school's star athlete but had since let himself go. His hair was thinning on top of his head, and his white tank top was food-stained, stretching over a large beer belly. Peter could see in Greg's eyes that he was half drunk. And for only eleven in the morning, it was concerning. A half drank bottle swayed in Greg's hand as he wiped his mattered beard with his other hand.

When Greg caught sight of Peter, his entire demeanor changed, as did Taylor's at her husband's arrival. Peter couldn't help but notice how she shrank when Greg raised his voice and how she appeared to cower when the door ripped open. This was obviously not a happy household. Was Greg an angry drunk? Had he killed Mr. Dalton while Taylor tried to frame Peter to protect her husband?

"Peter? Man, I haven't seen you in years. How have you been, buddy? Come here," Greg said, his face lighting up in a smile.

Pushing past his wife, Greg pulled a reluctant Peter into a hug. Greg's smell filled Peter's nostrils, and Peter struggled to keep his face vacant. Body odor, cigarette smoke, and beer were just a few of Greg's foul smells. This, a shocking contrast to the woman who stood over his shoulder, a woman who took pride in her appearance compared to her husband, who seemed to no longer care about his. Stained leftover food stuck to his mattered beard. Peter forced a smile.

"Good to see you, Greg," Peter lied, taking a small step back.

"What brings you to my place?" Greg asked, taking a swig of his beer.

"I've just come to ask Taylor about Mr. Dalton, see if I can shed some light on the situation," Peter answered.

"Oh yeah, right, you're a big fancy lawyer now, huh? Don't mind Taylor. She is always up in everyone's business and gets worked up about stupid things," Greg said, waving a dismissive hand in Taylor's direction.

Taylor clearly didn't like being dismissed and suddenly stood up straighter with a defiant look.

"Well, I don't think murder is stupid. That's why I handed the footage to the police," Taylor said proudly, as though she deserved a Nobel prize for citizen of the year.

Greg scoffed, waving another dismissive hand at his wife.

"Oh pish, Mr. Dalton was an old fool. No one murdered him. He probably slipped and bashed his head in on the stairs. We all know he was going crazy. Why do you think the school fired him in the first place?" Greg said, his half-drink state loosening his tongue.

"Fired? I heard he was forced to retire?" Peter enquired.

"Isn't that the same thing?" Greg laughed, his overly large belly jiggling as he did.

"Right," Peter said, about to give up.

Between Taylor refusing to give up information, she had already decided that Peter was guilty, and Greg's drunken state Peter wasn't going to find the answer he was hoping for. Preparing to leave and look for solutions elsewhere, Peter nodded softly and turned to go when something Greg said startled not just him but Taylor too.

"Or who knows, maybe that no good son of his finally did him in," Greg blurted out, stumbling and bashing his back against the door frame.

Taylor gasped, "I went to school with Todd. He wouldn't do such a thing," Taylor protested.

"Why are you so concerned all of a sudden?" Greg snapped at Taylor.

"I'm not; you just caught me off guard. I've had enough of this conversation now anyway," Taylor stormed off back inside, but Peter could see she had set up camp by the window, prepared to watch him leave.

Peter could sense that there was more to it than Taylor was admitting. Why else would she act so shocked by the accusation? Drunken words are sober thoughts. After all, perhaps Greg was speaking some sense. Peter decided that maybe a change in subject would offer more insight.

"Wow, anyway, Greg, how have you been? Last time I saw you, you were on track for a football scholarship," Peter said, slipping into buddy mode.

"Nah, busted my knee final year, didn't I? Oh well, what can you do, hey? Been working at the car dealership outside Pine Grove for years now," Greg said.

"You always did have a thing for cars," Peter chuckled.

"Yeh, but I was laid off a few months ago now. I don't know what else to do. The dealership had been my life," Greg muttered.

The atmosphere grew tense and solemn. Greg's eyes looked like they were glistening with tears. A man broken by life and struggling with his pride and failed dreams. Downing the rest of his drink in one gulp, Greg tossed the empty bottle onto the lawn outside his house. It was plain for all to see that, as a way to deal with his broken childhood dream, Greg had chosen a life of drowning his sorrows.

"Anyway, Peter, good to see you. We should meet for drinks some-time, have a guy's night for the old days," Greg said, running his hands over his face but keeping his gaze away from Peter.

"Sure, Greg, sounds good," Peter said, pity filling him seeing Greg's state.

"Cool, man, cool," Greg muttered, heading back inside.

Both men knew they would never meet up for drinks, but Peter worried that perhaps all Greg needed was a friend. Dissatisfied that he was no closer to figuring things out, Peter put his sights on other things. He still had his date with Jessica later that evening, and that was something he was much looking forward to.

CHAPTER
SEVEN

MYERS' *residence*

Jessica arrived just after six. She came straight from work, still wearing her white lab coat. Peter didn't mind, she still looked beautiful, and her smile lit up the room. The first course was a shrimp salad, which went down like a treat with the white wind Jessica brought along. Sam was defiantly happy to see her.

At first, Peter had to fight for Jessica's attention. Sam jumped all over her, licking her face and jumping in her lap for hugs. Peter struggled to get Sam to stop trying to join them at the table, shooing him off the spare seat several times and making Jessica laugh. Her laugh was warm, and it felt like a hug had filled the room. Peter never expected to feel a rush like it, but things with Jessica seemed so easy. Their conversation flowed and was never dull. But it wasn't long before the talk of the town buzz popped up.

News traveled fast in Pine Grove, and Taylor Logan had helped by fanning the flames and whispers. Soon the entire town was talking about Peter Myers, the big-shot lawyer now being investigated for murder.

Peter slapped three steaks on the grill, and Sam was swift on his heels. Slathering, knowing one of those juicy stakes was for him.

"Sam, calm down, boy," Peter insisted.

"Woof," Sam barked, his tail wagging manically.

"Sam," Jessica said, clicking her fingers.

Sam bounced across the room, happy to sit proudly at Jessica's side while she sipped her wine.

"He likes you. He responds well to you, too," Peter smiled.

"Well, the feeling is mutual, buddy," Jessica said to Sam, who barked back happily.

"I'm curious, how does someone like you get the town so a buzz?" Jessica asked, stroking the stem of her wine glass.

"Someone like me? I don't know if I should take that as an insult or a compliment," Peter joked.

"You know what I mean, someone so put together. I can't remember the last time someone set tongues wagging so much," Jessica laughed.

Peter appreciated that she was trying to make a joke out of the situation; it made it easier. Even though Peter knew he was innocent, he couldn't help but feel somewhat nervous. The police captain clearly had no clue what he was doing and was set on pinning the murder on Peter. There was also the fact that he couldn't get any sense out of Greg and Taylor, and with every rumor that met his ears, more questions arose. It appeared Taylor had spun enough of a tale around town that everyone had painted Peter as the villain: The sell-out who left town and came back only to murder a much-loved, innocent old teacher.

"The tongues wagging didn't stop you from coming for dinner," Peter pointed out.

"Maybe I'm curious if you killed the old man," Jessica laughed, giving Peter a little wink.

"What if I did? Are you not worried about what people might think of you choosing to dine with a murderer?" Peter asked.

"No. Some other news will pique their curiosity soon enough, and the vet's practice has been crazy lately, so even if business slows, I could use the break," Jessica said.

Peter shrugged in understanding.

"I'd be more worried about being murdered too, but ok," Peter mocked.

Jessica laughed, her laugh warming Peter's heart.

"IF you were going to kill me, I think you would have done it already," Jessica teased.

There was no avoiding the conversation. Avoidance would only make him look guilty. And Peter had nothing to hide. Jessica had been living in Pine Grove for the last few years, and the way gossip spread through the town, it would make sense that if anyone knew something about Mr. Dalton, Jessica would, especially since Peter had been out of town for so many years.

"Do you know anything about Mr. Dalton's son?" Peter asked.

He had tried digging but couldn't find much information on the wayward son. Taylor's reaction made his gut twist, thinking perhaps the son was more involved than he thought. What if Taylor and Dalton's son had an affair, and Mr. Dalton had found out? That would be motive enough for murder. Mr. Dalton could have threatened to tell Greg.

Jessica shook her head, taking another sip of wine.

"I didn't really know either of them, to be honest. I didn't go to school here, so I only know Mr. Dalton as the crabby old man who mumbles around town, or so the rumors call him. I always thought it was a cruel way to describe someone. Although, I did hear an owner of one of my patients say that Mr. Dalton's son is in town," Jessica realized.

"Really?" Peter asked, his curiosity piqued.

"Yeah, I remember now. They were talking to my boss. They said they were surprised he got here so quickly, considering he lives in Oregon. He works at a college or something, maybe as a teaching assistant or a sports coach? I can't exactly remember. But I remember thinking, it's the middle of the academic year. How could he leave like that?" Jessica answered, shrugging.

"Good point."

"Anyway, I can't imagine you invited me around to talk about the investigation, so how about a subject change?" Jessica offered.

"That would be greatly appreciated, thank you," Peter smiled.

The rest of the night went better than Peter had expected. With Jessica having patients early in the morning, she didn't stay too late, but that didn't mean the night wasn't fun. Being a gentleman, Peter didn't venture for a goodnight kiss. He respected Jessica and wanted the chance to get to know her better first. Everything he had seen so far, he liked. She was funny, strong-minded, and didn't care for idle gossip. Sam loved her, and she him. But even as his mind raced with thoughts of the evening, Jessica telling him Dalton's son was in town occupied his thoughts.

CHAPTER
EIGHT

DALTON RESIDENCE

Peter tried to rest, tossing and turning, knowing Mr. Dalton's murder needed an answer. Then, unable to leave well enough alone, He dressed in an all-black tracksuit and baseball cap and headed out.

"Woof!" Sam barked.

"Sorry, boy, you can't come with me. But I'll be back soon," Peter said, offering Sam a treat.

Peter parked around the corner from Mr. Dalton's house. He didn't want to be spotted by the fancy new doorbell camera. Creeping through the shrubbery around the house, Peter checked windows and doors. No one appeared to be inside, which was not surprising. Then, sneaking out back through the woods, using the torch on his phone, Peter searched for any clues that someone may have broken in or come out.

Bedded deep in the flower bed were boot prints, two sets. One was likely Mr. Dalton's, but to whom did the others belong? Peter followed the larger pair that traveled around the house, close to all the windows. Someone was watching Mr. Dalton.

Looks like the old man wasn't crazy after all. The poor guy was scared, and rightly so, Peter thought, heading to the back of the house.

If there were enough clues out the back that Peter had found that the police had missed, perhaps there was more inside. But breaking and entering was a crime. And if he were caught, it would only make him look even more guilty. But something told Peter the answers were inside that house.

He headed towards the creaky back door with the broken screen basing against the frame in the small fall night's breeze. Peter almost fell into a firepit. A fresh one. It wasn't from Mr. Dalton. He had been killed the day before. The ashes in the grate must have been only a couple of hours old. Something still burned; had the killer tried to discard evidence? Why hadn't the police seen this sooner?

Pulling his penknife from his pocket, Peter poked through the ashes, and that's when he saw a charred envelope. Pulling out the latex gloves from his pocket, mindful not to get his fingerprints on what could be vital evidence, Peter extracted the message from inside the envelope.

'I know what you did. Pay....'

The rest of the message was already burned away. So, was this why Mr. Dalton was so hard up for cash? Was he being blackmailed? And what had Mr. Dalton done that was so bad to make him think he couldn't go to the police? How long had the poor man been suffering?

I wonder if there are any more of these notes inside? Peter thought.

Quickly snapping pictures of the boot prints and the note he found for evidence to protest his innocence, Peter prepared to go inside when, suddenly, the kitchen light flared to life. Ducking down into the flower bed, Peter watched for a shadow, a figure in the window. A clue as to who was inside and why.

Who was home? Had the true killer returned to destroy evidence? Peter didn't know, but he had nowhere else to go and didn't mind waiting to find out.

CHAPTER
NINE

DALTON RESIDENCE

Peter followed the light as it traveled through the house. With each light turned off, another would spring to life in another room. All the curtains were shut tight; no matter how close Peter got, he couldn't see who was inside. Whoever it was traveled upstairs and stayed there for a while. Peter checked his watch. It was almost five in the morning, and Peter had been observing the house nearly all night. He felt frozen to the bone.

Mindful to stay out of sight of the doorbell camera, Peter crept around the house. If he couldn't see anyone inside, he could at least watch whomever it was leave. Hiding in the bushes, Peter kept a close eye on the street; he didn't want any other neighbors to see him. But he needed a clear line of sight to Mr. Dalton's front door.

Finally, a tall, dark-haired man crept out the front door around five-thirty. Careful not to make a noise, the man closed the door behind him and locked it. Whomever it was had to be close to Mr. Dalton if he had a key. Was this the elusive missing son?

Peter tried to venture closer, but it was too risky. Any closer and he would be seen. The tall stranger turned his back to Peter and pulled his hood over his head, hiding his face before he left. A Black Porsche 911 GT3 touring sports car sat right out front. It was a pretty impressive piece of machinery; Peter couldn't understand how he had missed it. The car was at least one hundred thousand dollars easy. Was this the blackmailer?

Just as the stranger went to get in, Taylor emerged from her house in jogging gear, her eyes locked on the stranger across the street. The stranger swiftly returned a short nod of acknowledgment as he got in his car. The man drove off, and Taylor popped on her headphones and jogged off in the opposite direction.

Did these two know each other? Had Taylor purposefully given the police the footage to try and frame Peter to get the spot life off her? Was his original theory about Todd and Taylor having an affair right? Then, finally, things started to make sense. Taylor and her designer clothes, the mystery man in the luxury car, and the blackmail note. Deciding he couldn't wait another minute, Peter jogged to his car and headed to the police station.

CHAPTER
TEN

PINE GROVE POLICE *Station*

As expected, the police station was quiet for that time of the morning. Charging right for the administration desk, Peter came across an officer who looked the least bit interested in being there.

"How can I help you?" asked the officer in the most unenthusiastic voice Peter had ever heard.

"I'm here to speak to the captain. Is he here?" Peter asked.

"He isn't in right now. Come back later," said the officer.

"Then call him and get him here. It is vital that I speak with him. It is regarding the Dalton case," Peter said a little more forcefully.

"Aren't you the guy accused of the murder?" asked the officer.

Looking closer, Peter could tell the officer was not long qualified. The young lad looked young enough to be fresh from the police academy.

"Can you just get the captain here?" Peter sighed, beginning to lose patience.

"Take a seat," huffed the officer picking up the phone to make a call.

Fifteen minutes later, the police captain walked into the station with large bags under his eyes, holding a cup of coffee from the gas station coffee machine on the edge of town.

"This better be important, Mr. Myers," the captain snipped, indicating Peter should follow him to the back.

"I wouldn't be here if it weren't," Peter answered.

The police captain led Peter to his office, closing the door and yawning loudly. His crinkled shirt was not fully tucked into his trousers, with the odd button done up in the wrong order.

"What is so important that I had to come in now?" the captain asked, sipping his bitter-smelling coffee as he sat opposite Peter at his desk.

"Do you have the autopsy report?" Peter asked.

"This is why you had me come down here? You have some nerve, Mr. Myers. You are interfering with a police investigation when you are already the prime suspect. I should book you for wasting police time," the captain snapped.

It was evident that the captain wasn't a morning person.

"I'm tired of your games, captain. You can't arrest me when you have nothing to go on. Do you have the autopsy report or not? I know my rights, and as a suspect, I have the right to know the details," Peter snapped.

"I have it somewhere," the captain frowned, searching through the chaos of papers and folders on his desk.

It was no wonder to Peter why the captain didn't seem to know what he was doing or get anything done when his desk was in such shambles. The man clearly didn't care about anything but himself. Peter couldn't understand how a man of the law could be so distant from his job.

"You haven't even looked at it, have you? I bet when you finally find that report, it will show the time of death was that night, proving my innocence. But, of course, it wouldn't surprise me if the footage from that time of night had been erased," Peter snapped.

Being a man who prides himself on putting bad guys behind bars, the captain's lack of enthusiasm and level of caring vexed Peter. It was rare that Peter was quick to anger, but something about the captain ticked all the boxes that angered Peter the most.

Scanning over several documents, the captain's face softened. He no longer looked angry to have been dragged to work in the early morning hours; he looked uneasy, almost embarrassed he had missed something so glaringly obvious.

"You are somewhat correct....the time of death was ten p.m.; our footage shows you leaving nine hours earlier......the footage from that time is...." the police captain stuttered.

"Gone?" Peter said, relaxing back in the chair and folding his arms across his chest.

Peter couldn't help looking as smug as he felt. He had known this police captain wasn't up to the job.

"Not gone; it appears the bad weather created power outages. Between the hours of nine-thirty and eleven-thirty, the doorbell camera glitched several times. Turning on and off again," the police captain reluctantly admitted.

"Or it was deliberately turned off," Peter suggested.

"Excuse me?" the captain asked, stunned he hadn't thought of it himself.

"I suggest you take a look at the Logans themselves, Taylor Logan in particular. And while you are at it, call in Todd Dalton, Mr. Dalton's son. I hear he is in town," Peter suggested rising to his feet.

"Todd Dalton is in town?"

"Yes, you may find it interesting that Greg Logan said perhaps Todd killed his father," Peter said.

Peter tossed his phone onto the table, preloaded with the pictures he had taken from the Dalton residence. The police captain's eyes widened in surprise.

"I don't want to tell you how to do your job, captain. But if I can find evidence in such obvious places, I don't know how you didn't. Footprints by the windows, a burning note in the backyard, and someone was at the house last night. Since you love doorbell cam footage so much, why not ask Taylor for the footage from half an hour ago? I'm sure it will shed some light on the situation," Peter said, grabbing his phone back and leaving without another word.

EPILOGUE

GOSSIP AROUND TOWN the following day was like fire spreading through a forest. No one could understand how Peter was cleared so easily and how the police captain had solved the crime. Apparently, Peter wasn't the only one to have noticed the captain's incompetence at times.

With the investigation no longer looming over his head and the answers to his questions finally answered, Peter could relax. No longer distracted by the prospect of going to prison for a crime he didn't commit, Peter invited Jessica out for a morning coffee.

They sat enjoying the gentle warmth of the October morning sun, both wrapped up in case of impending wind. Jessica had opted for a pumpkin spice latte; it was her favorite thing about fall, while Peter stuck to black coffee. Why mess with a classic?

"I'm in awe of the gossip surrounding us," Jessica smiled.

"Gossip?" Peter asked, intrigued.

"Yeah, the crazy vet willing to date a suspected murderer and the murder suspect who helped solve a crime."

"I haven't heard anyone suggest I helped solve it," Peter said.

"Well, they haven't, but I'm no fool. I know you had something to do with it. There is no way the police chief managed to solve it so quickly on his own. Let's say he has a reputation for taking credit for other people's work," Jessica winked.

Peter kept stumped, but his smug grin told Jessica all she needed to know.

"Go on then, tell me," Jessica said.

Peter explained how he and the police chief had discovered a foul plot afoot. The Logans and Todd Dalton had planned to kill Mr. Dalton together. When Greg had been laid off and Todd sacked for misconduct at the college in Oregon, the pair had met up when Todd came to town looking to get back into his father's good books.

"Back in his good books? What do you mean?" Jessica asked, enthralled with the details.

"Mr. Dalton and Todd had a falling out years ago, and Mr. Dalton had disowned his son, took him out of the Will, and stopped his inheritance," Peter answered.

"So, how were the Logans involved?"

Peter explained that Taylor and Todd went back years. And when she saw Todd with her husband, they concocted the blackmail plot.

"Ah, I see. So that explains why Taylor was suddenly sporting designer clothes and handbags," Jessica realized.

"And the new fancy doorbell that caught me leaving, she tried to use to pin the crime on me," Peter said.

"I'll admit, I never thought Taylor had it in her. She wasn't always the brightest bulb in the box," Jessica said, but not to be insulting. "So why kill him?"

"Once they rinsed the poor man dry, they were worried he would go the authorities about being watched. Everyone saw him with the shotgun. I mean, Mr. Dalton wasn't wrong. His son, a cruel man, was leaving blackmail notes where he would find them, kept the old man on edge for months," Peter tutted, feeling for Mr. Dalton.

"Did you find out what Dalton did? Wasn't he just a simple science teacher?" Jessica asked.

The answer was simple yet heartbreaking. Todd and the Logans had taken advantage of an old man's guilt and declining health.

"Todd's mother, Sylvia, had a lot of money; she was an heiress or something. Dalton inherited it all when she passed. Dalton blamed himself for not being there when she died, too busy working. He was never the same after that. Seeing his father's misplaced guilt and recognizing early onset Dementia, Todd saw how he could benefit since he was out of the Will."

"That's disgusting and heartbreaking. Poor Mr. Dalton," Jessica said, visibly upset by the tale.

Peter reached across the table, gently taking Jessica's hand. Instantly he felt a spark of electricity shoot through him, and from the look in her eyes, she had too.

"Let's change the subject to happier things," Peter smiled.

"I wish I could, but I better head off to work. Murder talk aside, this was fun," Jessica smiled gently, pressing her lips to Peter's cheek.

Jessica gave Sam a quick pat on the head and received a lick in thanks before she headed off to the vet clinic. Peter watched her leave. Like a schoolboy, he pressed his hand to his cheek. Jessica was something special.

"Woof! Woof! Woof!" Sam barked after her, a small sorrowful whimper at her departure, leaving his throat.

Peter wrapped his arms around Sam's neck, hugging the dog tightly.

"I know, boy, I'm sad to see her leave too, but who knows, maybe we will meet again soon," Peter hoped.

"Woof!" Sam barked in agreement.

Peter laughed softly at his four-legged friend, who brought so much joy into his life.

"Come on, boy. Let's go home," Peter smiled, leading the way.

Peter was in such a good mood that he decided to take the long way home. He wanted to enjoy the beauty of the crazy little town he called home. The mountains behind the town were framed by the stunning, ever-changing foliage of fall. The smell of the trees hung in the fall air. Even with a slight chill as winter approached, it was beautiful. Sam walked proudly at his side, Peter's new best friend. The few people around town who chose not to indulge in idle gossip waved and said hello. Peter waved back, wishing everyone a good day.

Life was beautiful; there was no way about it. But still, Peter had a sinking feeling that the blissful piece of Pine Grove would soon come to an end. What else did this tiny little town have in store for Peter and Sam? He had only been back at his family home for two months, the mayor was already cloaked in scandal, and Peter had been accused of murder.

Peter didn't dare ask the question of what else could go wrong; he did not want to scare or tempt fate. But one question he did want to ask was whether things would progress with Jessica. Her warm face, gentle eyes, and hearty laugh played in his memory. Dare Peter dream of a love connection? Either way, he was happy to have her in his life, whether as a love interest or just as a friend. He also knew that Sam loved her too, which meant he always had an excuse to see her.

Her gentle goodbye kiss still tickled his cheek, making Peter smile like a young boy again.

"She really is something, isn't she, boy?" Peter asked.

"Woof!" replied Sam, his tail wagging in agreement.

Without realizing it, Peter's mind wandered a little further to what his late mother would think of Jessica. His mother also loved animals. And knowing the type of person Jessica was, Peter was proud to say his mother would have loved her. It was such a shame that she had passed and never got a chance to meet her.

The End

The Feline Caper

A PINE GROVE MYSTERY

DAISY LANDISH

PROLOGUE

TIMMS RESIDENCE

A CHILL WIND pierced through Verna Timms, making her arthritic joints ache. Shadows built along the streets surrounding her backyard, sending a shiver down her spine. Pine Grove, New England, had once seemed the perfect place to retire. Verna felt good about residing close to her remaining family in a place she knew well.

"Persephone?" she called, rattling the bag of treats. Fall was near its end, and the nights were bitterly cold. "Persephone, where are you, baby?"

She strained her ears for a distant mewling, but there were no answering sounds. The rest of the cats twined around her feet, crying for their supper. It had taken her hours to round them all up. There was still no sight of the elegant Persephone.

Somewhere in the growing darkness, a dog barked. The yipping of coyotes answered. Verna shook the treat bag harder, hoping desperately that her cat would return. It wasn't safe out here. Verna was worried that something terrible had happened. Her heart ached whenever she thought of everything that could go wrong.

This can't be happening, she thought.

Some of her neighbors sneered at her, calling her everything from 'crazy cat lady' to 'hoarder.' But she wasn't—yes, she had a lot of cats in her care. She had fostered a poor kitty many times until it could move on to its forever home. She only kept the ones nobody else wanted.

Ever since her dear husband had passed on, Verna had been rescuing cats nobody else would take. Blind, missing limbs, or angry, spitting cats. Every one she brought into her home got warmth, love, and food.

She meticulously cleaned out the various litter boxes in the house every day and spent hours sweeping, vacuuming, and cleaning. She even had her nephew come around to help her build a safe enclosure in the backyard so her kitties could enjoy the outdoors without being in danger from passing cars or predators.

The little black cat named Hades placed his paws on her knee, letting out an extra plaintive yowl. Helplessness swept through Verna.

"Persephone," she called one last time.

Nothing. Darkness was growing even thicker around her, and she reluctantly turned back to her house. She was angry but also worried. This couldn't have been an accident. But she couldn't bear to think about anyone deliberately hurting her kitties.

Verna opened the door, letting the cats stream back into its warmth. Only Hades stayed out. He stared with pricked-up ears, and his tail flicked back and forth to the property line.

Verna hobbled toward the fence. "Persephone?"

Hades' fur stood on end, and he hissed. The wind picked up, bringing more cries from coyotes with it. At the edge of town, backed onto a land conservation as she was, Verna was reminded that the wildlife was never very far away. Tears pricked her eyes as she shook the bag in one last desperate attempt to entice Persephone back.

Nothing.

She turned and swooped Hades into her arms. Cuddling him to her chest, she hurried inside and shut the door. As the warmth of her home thawed her bones, Verna prayed that, wherever she was, Persephone would survive the night.

CHAPTER
ONE
MAIN STREET, PINE GROVE

PETER LIFTED his face to the glowing sun, reveling in the strange burst of summer-like conditions the day offered. Despite the frosty nights, the daytime was pleasant. Add in the colorful hues of the New England fall hanging on, his usual morning jog had been exceptionally enjoyable, even this close to winter.

"Woof!" While trotting at this side, Sam wagged his tail as he attempted to catch a falling leaf.

Peter smiled at his dog. It wasn't just the weather that put him in such a good mood. The kind vet, Dr. Jessica Stern, who helped him out with Sam, was meeting them for lunch at the café on main street. With such a beautiful day, they had already taken advantage of the open patio.

As Peter approached, however, he was surprised to see Jessica wasn't alone. An older woman with greying hair sat at the table beside her. The woman's hands were cupped around a black mug, while Jessica had a mug herself that was pushed to one side. She patted the woman's arm, her brows pinched together.

Jessica was always ready to greet Peter with a smile. Seeing her like this upset him. Questions raced through his mind. What was going on?

He stepped up to the table and cleared his throat. Both Jessica and the older woman jumped. Looking closer, he saw this woman wearing a midnight blue floor-length dress. A shawl was wrapped around her shoulders, and her short grey hair was styled impeccably. She was clearly a woman who took pride in her appearance, even if her fashion sense was somewhat dated.

"Peter, I'm glad you're here." Jessica smiled at him, but it seemed strained.

"Woof!" Sam wagged his tail as he trotted under the table to put his head in the older woman's lap. His nose twitched, and he licked her hand.

The old woman gave the dog a watery smile. "You're a real sweetheart, aren't you?"

Peter took his seat and tied Sam's leash to the chair.

"Verna, this is my friend Peter," Jessica said, nodding toward him. "He's brilliant at solving knotty problems. I'm sure he can help with this."

Verna turned toward him and squinted. "Ah, yes. The Myers boy. Everyone's talking about how you solved poor Mr. Dalton's murder when that incompetent Captain Donnelly was too busy being a... well, some things a lady should not say, even when they're true."

Peter had to bite back a laugh. With the way Sam responded to her and her way of talking, he was quickly finding he liked Verna. "What seems to be the problem at hand?"

Verna took a deep, shuddering breath, but it appeared she couldn't speak. She turned to Jessica.

With a sigh, Jessica explained. "Verna runs a cat sanctuary and fosters strays out of her home. She takes in any abandoned cats she can from the shelter. She works to get them back into peak health, and if she can find new homes for them, she does so. If they cannot be adopted for whatever reason, she keeps them until they pass on."

"That sounds admirable," Peter drawled. He was confused about what the problem was. "Is there a problem with your cats?"

"Three have gone missing in the last three weeks," Verna said. Her voice shook like she was on the verge of tears. Sam whined, and she rubbed his ears fondly.

Sam must not be bothered by cats, Peter thought. Verna must smell like them.

"I'm sorry that they're missing, but cats go missing all the time," Peter said.

Verna shook her head firmly. "I take good care of my cats. I don't allow them to go wandering around the neighborhood. They'd get eaten by coyotes or hit by cars. Not to mention the number of cruel people who would torment and kill them for no reason."

Peter frowned. "Then how are they going missing?"

"That's what we're worried about," Jessica sighed.

"The police are ignoring me entirely. My cats all got out yesterday, and I do not know how. I keep the doors and windows shut. I have an enclosure in my backyard for them, and the police keep saying that I must have left the door open, but I know I didn't."

Peter folded his hands on the table. He wasn't sure exactly what Jessica thought he could do about this. Even if Verna insisted that she couldn't have accidentally let her cats out, there could be many things that she could have overlooked, especially if it had happened three times already.

Before Peter could say anything, though, the server came over. He was chewing a piece of gum, smacking his lips obnoxiously as he asked, "Do you want anything?"

Peter frowned. He'd never been treated so rudely here before. "I'll get a cup of coffee."

"Fine. But you better all clear out soon. I hate cats." The server eyed Verna with disgust.

Sam growled.

"Hush, Sam," Peter said, and Sam fell silent. He faced the server. "A cup of coffee, and if we are being kicked out, please let your manager do it rather than taking it on yourself. Besides, I don't see any cats here. Do you?"

The server wrinkled his nose and stomped over to a table at the other end of the patio. The woman who sat there was glaring at him, Verna, and Jessica. Another cat-hater, perhaps? It was ridiculous. Yes, it appeared Verna was in some ways the typical 'cat lady,' but she was well-groomed and articulate, and there wasn't a trace of cat hair on her.

Something in his gut told Peter there was more to this story after all. He was ashamed of himself for jumping to conclusions already. Between the apparent hostility from the server and the woman in the corner, he was getting the feeling that something was up.

"Can you tell me about the cats?" Peter asked.

Verna shifted in her seat, her eyes growing misty. "First, it was Ares. He was always a fighter, a scrappy little guy who had had it rough in life. He was feral growing up and was never fully comfortable inside. I can understand him finding some escape route and taking off. That was three weeks ago."

Peter nodded.

"Then, last week, Hera disappeared. She was always curious and loved to spend time in the 'catio,' the enclosure in my backyard," Verna explained. "She took every opportunity she could to get out my front door and play in the yard, but she never went past the fence and always came for treats."

Jessica gave Peter a significant look as though they were just getting to the part where the tale got suspicious.

"And the third one?" Peter pressed.

"Yesterday, when I came home from volunteering at the library, I saw that the catio was open. All the cats were gone. I searched for hours and got back all twelve, except Persephone."

Peter's eyes widened. "Twelve? You have twelve cats?"

"For the time being," Verna said.

Jessica reached to pat her shoulder comfortingly. "We've had a lot of abandoned animals come into the clinic lately. People treat cats like throwaway pets and just dump them on the side of the road."

Peter still thought that was an awful lot. "But is it even legal to have that many cats?"

"I have special permission from the city," Verna said, sounding put out. "I am a sanctuary and foster, after all."

"Right." Peter nodded, feeling a little chagrinned. Even so, twelve cats? How did she take care of them all?

Verna's lip trembled, but she straightened her shoulders and continued. "Persephone is a beautiful old Persian cat. She's twenty years old."

"Persians normally live twelve to seventeen years," Jessica murmured.

An ancient cat, then. She must be well taken care of.

Verna stroked her thumb across Sam's head. "Persephone hated going outside. She even refused the catio. She liked sitting on her pillow in the front window and watching the birds or napping in the sunshine."

"Can we count on you to look for her?" Jessica asked, her eyes never leaving Peter's face.

"I can't promise I'll find anything out. But I'll do my best," Peter promised. "Something about this just doesn't add up."

CHAPTER
TWO
POLICE STATION

CAPTAIN DONNELLY LOOKED like he was ready to kick Peter out before Peter even said a word. As Peter entered, he sat behind his desk with an annoyed look on his face. Though his hands were folded over a file folder, Peter caught the reflection of a TV show from the captain's computer screen on the framed photograph behind him.

"What do you want, Myers?" Donnelly snapped.

Peter sat in the chair across from Donnelly. He wasn't about to let the man intimidate him. From the years he worked with the FBI as a lawyer, Peter had seen that tactic used far too often. The best way to deal with a blustering type of police officer like this was to remain calm and in control.

"I'm here to ask you if you've looked into the reports of missing animals from Verna Timms," Peter said.

Donnelly stared at him before he burst into laughter.

Peter frowned. "What exactly is so funny?"

"That crazy old cat lady has you running as her errand boy, has she?" Donnelly asked. He slapped his knee, still laughing. "No, I haven't looked into any missing cat reports. Who cares? They're just cats."

Peter felt himself bristling and fought his anger down. He had always preferred dogs over cats, but he understood why people like Verna would love them. Right now, he was strongly reminded of Jessica telling him cats were 'throw away' animals. No creature deserved to be treated that way.

Peter knew he would not get anywhere appealing to Donnelly's humanity. So, he went for a different approach. "Aren't you at all concerned that the missing animals might indicate that someone is breaking into Mrs. Timms' house?"

"You might be from here, but you've been gone too long, Myers." Donnelly clasped his hands over his belly, smiling as he leaned back in his chair.

He was baiting Peter, trying to get under his skin. But Peter would not let him have the pleasure. He arched an eyebrow at the captain. "And what do you mean by that?"

"What I mean is that Old Timms is a crazy cat lady. I'm not wasting my time or police resources trying to find her missing cats just because she's so old and crazy that she can't remember to shut the door."

Peter reflected on the fact that every time he came to this station, his opinion of Donnelly and the police working here grew even lower. "You really think it's something like that? She seems to be mentally sound to me."

Donnelly rolled his eyes. "If you have too much time on your hands, why don't you take that mutt of yours and go hunting for the cats yourself?"

"Have you even looked at her house? Done any sort of investigation?"

"You're wasting my time." Donnelly grabbed a pencil and started scribbling on the papers before him.

It was clear Peter would not get anything from him. Donnelly was already watching his TV show when Peter shut the door to his office.

Peter headed outside, frustrated and angry from being dismissed. The way Donnelly talked about Verna and her cats was so callous! It was terrible. Clearly, Jessica and Peter were the only ones who cared about the situation.

Once in his car and heading home, Peter decided he would have to do some research on cats. Mainly, he needed to know just how far a cat would roam. And why would an elderly cat who preferred her days napping in the sunshine, not wanting to step outside, suddenly disappear into the unknown world?

CHAPTER
THREE
MYERS RESIDENCE

SAM LAY on his bed in the kitchen, stretched out with his paws pointed in the air. Though he appeared to be sleeping, Peter occasionally caught his eyes winking open in the stove's general direction. Peter had to laugh.

"I think Sam knows we're cooking a steak for him," he said to Jessica.

Jessica was at the long counter, making her famous bacon guacamole. Even though Sam was getting a steak today, the humans had decided on taco night. Peter thought about how Sam had gotten very used to having food for himself when Peter had his supper.

"You don't think I'm developing bad habits in him, do you?" Peter asked worriedly.

Jessica laughed. "Look at him, lying there all calm and serene. Bad habits would be if he were getting underfoot or begging. He's a good boy. Aren't you Sam?"

Sam lifted his head and wagged his tail. "Woof," he said in agreement.

Jessica tossed him a small piece of bacon. Sam sniffed it and looked at Peter.

"Oh, look. He's asking for permission," Jessica said.

"Go ahead," Peter said.

Sam wagged his tail again and licked the bacon off the floor. Peter smiled proudly at him. Sam was a wonderful dog. Peter wouldn't have ever thought he would have such a delightful companion when he first saw the thin, abused dog in the forest. But Sam had proven himself many times over.

"Have you made any discoveries in Verna's case?" Jessica asked as she put the rest of the bacon into the guacamole.

Peter winced. He had been dreading this conversation ever since he had finished his research. "I'm not sure. I researched cats and talked to a couple of Verna's neighbors."

Jessica set the bowl aside and leaned against the counter, staring at him.

Peter flipped Sam's steak. It was almost done. "If I'm honest... I'm not sure there is a case here at all."

"Why not?" Jessica's tone was strained.

"Well..." Peter was hesitant to explain his findings. Though he was pretty certain there wasn't more to this situation than he had already found, he also didn't want to disappoint Jessica. He liked her and hated to let her down.

Jessica turned fully to him and folded her arms. "Well, what? You can tell me, Peter. I'm a big girl."

"The truth is, I don't think there is much of a case at all," Peter admitted.

Disappointment filled Jessica's eyes.

"I'm sorry," Peter said, hating to have to say all this. "It's not that I don't believe something is happening. I just don't think there is anything nefarious."

"All right. What do you think is happening, then?" Jessica's voice was still strained.

Peter took the steak off the stove to let it cool before feeding it to Sam. As it rested on the plate, he carried their taco toppings to the kitchen table. He wasn't sure how he was going to tell Jessica his suspicions.

"First, let's talk about Ares and Hera, the first two cats that went missing. Verna said that Ares was an outdoor cat that hated to be inside. It makes sense that he'd take off if he had the chance."

Jessica helped carry the fixings over to the kitchen. "Yes, but Verna is always careful. She never let them out except in the enclosed catio."

"There are many ways a determined cat could find a way out of the house," Peter pointed out. He went back to the steak and cut it into strips for Sam. "Verna has twelve cats. It can't be easy to keep track of all of them."

Jessica shook her head. "She takes too good care of them for Ares to have just gotten out because she wasn't paying attention."

"I didn't say that," Peter insisted. "I only meant that if he didn't want to be there, he could have left without her noticing. Cats can be sneaky."

Jessica opened the fridge and pulled out a pitcher of water. "And Hera?"

"Verna said she liked to find ways out of the house and hang out in the backyard, correct?"

"Yes."

Peter nodded. "Then she probably got out—perhaps the same way Ares did—and either roamed or was taken by an animal from the yard, or even some misguided human who thought she was being abused took her home with them."

"I… suppose," Jessica said doubtfully.

"From my research, cats can roam up to two and a half miles from home and will go hide somewhere to die." Peter hated bringing this up. Verna clearly loved her cats. "You said Persephone had outlived her normal lifespan already."

Jessica shook her head emphatically. "No. She hated being outside and wouldn't have left 'to go die.' She would have wanted to be comfortable. I'm her vet, and she was in perfect health. Much better condition than many cats younger than her."

"Jessica—"

"You talked to Verna's neighbors but didn't go to see her house yourself?" Jessica put her hands on her hips, her eyes crackling with irritation.

"I—" Peter cut himself off, chagrinned. He had no excuse.

"If you just went to her house and saw everything there, you would know. Verna is a sweet lady, and despite what you saw at the café, people like her."

"I guess I'm acting a bit like Donnelly, aren't I?" Peter admitted. "I'm sorry."

The tension in Jessica's shoulders melted away. "So, you'll look into it more?"

"Yes."

Jessica smiled at him. "Thank you."

"Sure thing," Peter said. He still wasn't convinced anything was happening, but Jessica was right. He couldn't just dismiss Verna so easily.

He pulled a chair for Jessica and put Sam's steak on the floor.

"I'll go see her tomorrow," he promised.

CHAPTER
FOUR
TIMMS RESIDENCE

PETER LET OUT a heavy breath as he pulled to a stop in the quiet cul-de-sac Verna Timms lived on. He took a moment to gaze around the neighborhood, getting his bearings. It was clear these buildings were older but were all well-cared for. The yards were neatly trimmed, and the trees had all lost their leaves to prepare for winter. Most yards were empty, but a few already had blow-up Christmas decorations.

Verna's house was at the end of the cul-de-sac. From Peter's research, he knew her property was against a land conservatory. That explained the wide field behind the house, edged by a forest a quarter-mile away. Coyotes were a common site in this area. Not a safe place for cats.

Peter shook his head as he stepped out of his car. He hadn't told Jessica, but he had heard from one of Verna's neighbors that they had seen Verna leaving the doors to her house open more and more lately.

Unfortunately, no matter how much Verna loved her cats, her mental facilities could suffer here as she grew older. Peter was uncomfortable knowing he might be investigating a case of early-onset dementia or Alzheimer's.

He wasn't sure what would be worse, one of those diseases or if someone really was stealing her cats.

The front porch was screened in, and as he approached, Peter saw a pitch-black cat on its bed, cleaning its fur. Another cat, a grey-and-white shorthair, sat in the window, watching him with a grumpy expression.

Twelve cats.

Peter grimaced as he opened the screen door. There was a lock on it, but it appeared to be broken. The black cat bolted for the house as soon as he opened the door, disappearing through a square cat flap.

Closing the screen door behind him, Peter moved across the porch to ring the doorbell. He braced himself, preparing for what he was sure he was going to find.

Verna answered a minute later. "Hello, Peter. I'm glad you could come. Come in."

"Thank you," Peter smiled at her as he stepped inside.

To his surprise, the house was spotless. There was no sign of cat hair anywhere, and it had no cat smell at all. The house didn't have that musty sort of scent that came with a lot of elderly people's belongings, either. It seemed Verna took excellent care of her house.

The black cat jumped onto a hall table, batted at Peter's hand, and then jumped off and ran to Verna's feet.

"You'll have to excuse Hades," Verna said as she picked up the black cat and put him on her shoulder. "He comes from a situation where he was terribly abused by a man. It's given him trust issues."

"Understandable," Peter said, thinking about Sam. Anger ran through him. He couldn't understand why anyone would abuse an animal. "Do you have a cleaner?"

Verna led him through the living room. Cats were everywhere, on the windowsill, chairs, and tables. She even had shelves that ran along the ceiling where cats played. They all seemed so pampered and happy.

"Two cleaners," Verna said. "I have them come in on alternating days to help me around the house in case I need to have them come in and take care of my cats."

"Could they forget to close the doors?"

Verna shook her head. "No. I trust them implicitly."

"And you never find that you've forgotten to close or lock the doors?"

"Never."

"What about your porch screen door? I noticed the lock was broken," Peter said cautiously.

Verna's shoulders slumped. "Again? My goodness! I don't understand; I just replaced it the other day."

Peter filed that away in his mind as Verna continued to show him around the house. From what he saw, it was doubtful that the cats had just wandered out. As he talked with Verna, he continued to be impressed with her. He had to admit his concerns that her mental facilities might fail seemed far off.

"What did you do for work before you retired?" Peter asked politely, checking one window. It was locked tight.

"I did government work in D.C. I believe you did as well?" Verna asked. Hades had left, and a sphinx wearing a knitted sweater was now in her arms.

Peter looked at her in a new light. "Government work?"

Verna smirked. "Yes. What did you expect?"

"Not that." Peter thought about it for a moment and smiled at her. "I owe you an apology. I came in with preconceived notions, and I'm ashamed of my behavior."

"I'm used to it, Peter. It's a rare man who can admit when he's wrong."

Peter nodded at her, grateful she was so gracious. "Do you think that your disappearing cats could be connected to your old work? Someone is sending you a message?" he asked.

Verna's gaze darkened. "I have considered that. I hope it's not the case."

"What did you do?"

"Oh… just worked," Verna said, suspiciously vague. She waved a hand. "Let's go out. Come around back; you can check the catio."

The cats followed them as Verna pulled on her coat. She opened the back door, and the cats swarmed around her feet, meowing. She grabbed a bag of treats and tossed them around the impressive enclosure. The cats dashed this way and that having a great time chasing the treats.

"The cat flap to the screen door," Peter started. "Could the cats be escaping through that?"

"I lock it up at night to make sure they can't," Verna replied.

It wasn't big enough for a person to sneak through anyway. Peter examined the catio, but the screens were firmly secured to the frame. Several heated houses sat here and there, allowing the cats to stay warm at night.

"There has been no damage to the catio?" he pressed.

"No. I don't let them come out here at night anymore, either, not since Ares disappeared. I was worried about coyotes breaking in somehow."

Peter hummed, thinking this through. "Would Persephone have left the house if lured by a stranger? For meat, perhaps?"

Verna shook her head. "Never. She loved to sit in her window but cared little about anything else. If someone tried to lure a cat out with food, Hermes would have been the first out the door. But he's right here."

She lifted the sphinx in her arms.

"I don't get it," Peter muttered, running a hand through his hair. "What is going on here?"

CHAPTER
FIVE
PINE GROVE CENTENNIAL PARK

IT WAS another beautiful fall morning, although frost lingered on the ground. There was a nip to the air, but it quickly faded as the sun rose. Peter entwined his fingers with Jessica's as they walked through centennial park in the center of Pine Grove.

"I love this place," Jessica said, breathing in the wind.

"It's sure beautiful," Peter agreed.

The park had a small pond where ducks and geese liked to winter, fed by the people who came to the park and tossed out various grains, berries, and other tasty things. Several boxes were set up along the path filled with their feed and warnings that bread would cause the birds to be malnourished.

Sam tugged on his leash, whining as his head swung this way and that, searching the pond. Peter tugged lightly, bringing Sam back to his side. Jessica was walking a big Newfoundland dog that had surgery a few days ago. The large animal was gentle and welcoming to Sam, who had been nervous about her at first. They seemed to get along better now, though.

"Thanks for joining me on this walk," Jessica said. "Mindy needs to get moving more, and she just won't go for walks unless there's another dog with us."

Peter stroked Sam's head. "It's my pleasure. I certainly think Sam needs some more four-legged friends. I think he forgets he's a dog."

Peter wondered when Jessica would get to the real reason she had asked him specifically to come. They'd had little time to talk ever since their taco night. Peter still had little to share about the case. He was almost positive that Jessica was right and that something was going on. He just wasn't sure where to go from here, though.

"Do you want to get a cup of coffee and a late breakfast?" he offered. "We never got our lunch date."

Jessica laughed brightly. "Hey, but we had dinner. Doesn't that count as a makeup date?"

"Not when you have to make it yourself," Peter said wisely. He winked at her.

Jessica's cheeks turned pink, but she nodded.

They dropped Mindy off at the vet's office, and since Sam seemed to want to spend more time with the larger dog, they left him with her.

Peter and Jessica went to the café and took a seat on the patio.

"So," Jessica leaned her chin into her palm. "Are we going to get to the real reason you asked me to breakfast?"

"You mean the case?"

"You've been pussyfooting around it all morning," Jessica said. Her eyes twinkled. "Pun intended. But you've been waiting for me to bring it up, haven't you?"

Peter chuckled. Jessica could read him like a book. "Does Verna have any relatives in town?"

"She was never married, and the cats are her only children." Jessica tapped her fingers against the table. "I think she might have mentioned a nephew once or twice, but I don't really remember. From what I know, she didn't have any family at all."

"I see." Peter waved a server over. He was relieved to see it wasn't the same rude young man who had served them the last time they were here.

His mind turned over this new information. So, Verna didn't have any close relatives. That, combined with her cagey behavior when he asked her what work she had been in, showed something intense. Something that left her with either no time for a husband and children… or a job that made it unsafe for anyone to be in her immediate circle.

It was a sobering thought.

Peter pushed that thought from his mind, considering other options. "How did Verna get permission to have so many cats, anyway? I couldn't find any information about opening up a sanctuary in the middle of town as she has."

"What does that matter?" Jessica asked, her eyebrows furrowed.

"Well, if someone thinks she's mistreating them or is in a hoarding situation, they could steal the cats; I'm just trying to cover all the angles. She is an official sanctuary, isn't she?"

"Yes," Jessica snapped.

Peter held up his hands. "I'm not trying to accuse her of anything. I'm getting my facts straight."

Jessica sighed. "Sorry for my tone. Verna is a beautiful soul with a lot of heart and takes excellent care of those animals. But there are people in this town who are just… jerks."

"I'm sorry. I understand this has to be hard."

Jessica squeezed his hand. "Thanks for understanding. Yes, Verna is an official sanctuary. She was already established long before I came to Pine Grove. She's been having more problems since that new subdivision was built across from the cul-de-sac."

Peter made a mental note to check if any new neighbors had moved into the area in the last three weeks.

"Verna has to have a house inspection once a year to keep her status," Jessica said. Her eyes grew worried as she lowered her voice. "Her inspection is coming up; if the cats keep going missing, she might get closed down."

"Closed? But what will happen to the cats?"

Jessica shuddered. "Well, she can try to adopt them out. But they're all animals nobody else wanted. The chances are… they'll all be euthanized."

Peter's stomach clenched. There was more at stake than he had realized. *I have to figure this out and help Verna keep her sanctuary running. Otherwise…*

CHAPTER
SIX
MYERS RESIDENCE

ONCE HE WAS HOME, Peter called his old colleague at the FBI, Tiff. She answered after only a few rings.

"Hey, Peter," Tiff greeted. "What can I do for you?"

"I need some information on a woman in town by the name of Verna Timms," he said.

There was a choking sound on the other end. "Verna Timms? Are you serious? Why?"

Peter was surprised that she knew the name, let alone sounding so shocked and awed. He frowned as he pinched his cell phone between his shoulder and ear. "Because she's involved in a case I've been asked to look into."

"Verna Timms... involved in one of your cases? Does that mean she lives in Pine Grove?" Tiff sounded excited now.

Peter grabbed the mail off his kitchen table, where he had left it. All bills. "I do not know what you're talking about, Tiff. Who is she?"

"Only the best of the best of the best in the agency," Tiff replied, sounding almost affronted now. "You worked for years; how did you never hear about her? She's a legend! A myth! An inspiration to half the junior agents who come in. She's been retired for something like twenty years, and her name is still spoken in hushed whispers."

Peter tossed the bills back on the table and moved to the fridge, checking the milk. "Sorry. She's not ringing a bell."

"Maybe this will. Ever heard of Shadowcat?"

Peter nearly dropped both the milk and the phone. He had to catch both, shoving the milk back into the fridge as he did so. He put the phone back to his ear. "Shadowcat? You're telling me that Verna Timms is Shadowcat?"

Tiff laughed, sounding pleased. "So, you have heard of her!"

"Of course!"

He had never met the agent whose code name was Shadowcat, but Tiff was right. She was spoken of in awe. She was well-known for her ability to slip in and out of seemingly impossible missions, with no one being the wiser. Rumor had it she had brought in more criminals than any other agent.

"And she's in Pine Grove?" Tiff asked again, sounding excited.

"Yes."

"But she's having trouble?"

Peter considered the situation. He doubted an agent like Shadowcat would want her dirty business broadcasted. "No, no. I just needed some information. This has cleared up a lot. Thanks, Tiff."

"Anytime."

Peter hung up and tapped his cell phone against his bottom lip, considering the situation. Knowing this, he had to get more information from Verna.

I could have used this from the start, he thought as he grabbed his keys. Sam was snoozing on the couch, and Peter left him there; he shouldn't be too long.

Was this Agency business? Had she talked to the people back at the Agency to tell them she might be targeted? If not, why hadn't she? If these disappearing cats were some sort of revenge, taking out her children, how was he supposed to figure it out?

He jumped into his car and headed back to town. He was going to get answers, one way or another.

The Timms Residence

When Peter got to the cul-de-sac, it was dusk. A harsh wind blew in from the empty field, and Peter could already hear the yipping and howling of coyotes in the forest.

Verna's house was utterly dark. The screen door on the patio was wide open, and several cats were wandering down the stairs and back up, yowling and meowing in distress. Peter leaped from his car, his gut clenching. Something was wrong.

He hurried inside, finding the front door unlocked. He turned on a light, and all the cats that had been out on the porch streamed in. Their meows became more urgent. Peter shut the door and found the cat flap was locked.

Someone had driven the cats out and then locked them outside.

"Verna?" he called, heart hammering.

No response. Peter searched the house, but there was no sign of her anywhere. Out the back, the catio had had several screens ripped out. Peter shut and locked the cat flap that led out there. All the cats were staring at him, silent now.

The black cat, Hades, darted forward. He swiped at Peter's shoelace, then bolted for a doorway. He clawed at it, meowed loudly, and raced back at Peter.

Peter hurried over and opened the door. It led to a staircase going down into the basement.

And at the base of the stairs, in a crumpled, bleeding heap, was Verna.

CHAPTER
SEVEN
PINE GROVE HOSPITAL

"BUT MY CATS," Verna insisted.

Jessica, standing next to Peter, folded her arms. "No, you don't have to worry about them. I stopped in earlier and have already made sure they're taken care of for the night. You just worry about yourself."

Verna huffed. The bandage over her eyebrow had a small dark spot right in the middle, but luckily, she hadn't bled too much. Fortunately, she didn't have any broken bones. The doctors suspected she had a concussion. Since she was a little confused and disoriented, they kept her overnight.

Peter thought the staff would have to keep on their toes if they were going to keep her here. Verna was one stubborn woman.

Peter moved a little closer and touched Jessica's elbow. The last thing Verna needed was to be interrogated, but he still needed information. Convincing Jessica to help him had been difficult; in the end, though, she had agreed.

Now, she gave him a small, unhappy look. He nodded once.

Jessica squeezed Verna's hand. "Do you have any family I can call? You mentioned a nephew once, I think?"

"Oh, you don't have to bother him," Verna said quickly.

Peter leaned forward slightly. "So, you have a nephew?"

"Oh, yes. He's a dear, sweet soul. Few people can see that, though," Verna said sadly.

"Maybe I can call him, get him to stay with you?" Jessica suggested.

"No, no. He's a bit of a rough sort. He wouldn't exactly fit into a small place here in Pine Grove. My brother's son and my brother... well, he wasn't an exemplary parent. I tried my best to help my nephew out but there's only so much an aunt can do, especially when I was barred contact for years." Verna shook her head sadly.

Peter didn't like the sound of this. As her only living relative, this nephew had the potential to inherit everything. Could he have attacked her, wanting her house?

Verna's sharp eyes focused on his face. "Oh, no. I can see what you're thinking on your face. No, my nephew would never do something like this. He might have had it rough, but since my brother died, he's done his best to turn a corner. My nephew is a good boy if only he'd have the chance to prove it."

"Taking care of you while you're in recovery would be a chance," Peter pushed.

Verna shook her head. "No, no. He has a little bit of a temper, and with how the neighbors talk, he'd be bound to lose it." She mustered up a smile. "I will just get my things and head home."

"Verna," Jessica shook her head. "No. Stay the night."

"I don't have to do anything, young lady."

Peter ran a hand through his hair. "Jess, can I talk with her alone for a minute?"

Jessica hesitated. "Are you sure?"

"Oh, dear!" Verna gave a bright, hardy laugh. "Jessica, you don't have to worry over me. If Peter wants to speak with me, I will speak with him. Be a dear and get me a glass of water?"

Jessica didn't look very convinced, but she nodded. Before she left, though, she gave Peter a significant look. Even though they hadn't known each other for long, he understood it entirely.

Jessica was worried about Verna and didn't want Peter to push her too hard. Peter gave her a reassuring smile. During his years as a lawyer, he had learned how to gently interrogate a person to find what they were hiding without hurting them.

Once the vet was gone, Peter sat next to Verna's bed. "What happened?"

"I fell down the stairs. I've already told you that."

"I'm sorry, Verna, but I don't believe you." He kept his voice soothing. "I know you were part of the Agency. I know you took on tough cases and must have made enemies."

Verna shook her head. "I fell. That's all."

"When I came to your house, the cats were locked outside. You would never have done that." Peter looked deep into her eyes. "Someone pushed you, didn't they?"

"I…" Verna touched her forehead. "Oh, I'm so very dizzy. I can't—"

Peter held up a hand. "Please. I know when a person is faking an injury. That bump is real, but you're avoiding the question."

"Nobody pushed me." Verna dropped her hand, her kindly eyes narrowing. "I fell. That's all there is to it."

Was she protecting someone? Or was she trying to keep him out, so she could exact her own revenge against the perpetrator? Either way, Peter understood he would not get any more information.

He stopped by the water cooler to tell Jessica he was leaving and to ask her not to leave Verna alone. Jessica agreed.

Just as he was leaving the hospital, his phone rang. It was Tiff, and she didn't bother saying hello when he answered.

"Bad news," she said, sounding worried. "I looked into Shadowcat some more to see if I could find something. She worked on the McNulty case."

"McNulty?" Peter repeated.

"Francis and Felix McNulty were brothers. Verna brought them in and got them put away after she tracked down a lot of different crimes connected to them. Francis died only a few months ago, stabbed in the kidneys during a prison fight."

"And Felix?" Peter asked an uncomfortable feeling that he knew what she was going to say in his gut.

"He was released three weeks ago."

Right when the first cat disappeared. It seemed clear to Peter what was happening. Felix McNulty was out of prison… and going after Verna Timms for revenge.

"There's been a lot of calls made to her house," Tiff continued. "An unlisted number, but it's the same one every week, like clockwork. Maybe it's someone who knows what's going on?"

"Give it to me," Peter said.

One way or another, he had to figure this out. Before, whoever pushed Verna down the stairs tried to kill her again.

CHAPTER EIGHT

ON PETER'S way back to Verna's house, he called the number Tiff had given him. If whoever was calling Verna was harassing her, he had to find out who it was. The town was dark and dead at this time of night, without another car on the road.

The phone rang out until it hit a voice-answering message. No name was given by the robotic voice. Peter hung up and called again. This time, someone answered after five rings.

"What?" a male voice said from the other side, sounding irritated.

Wait, Peter knew that voice. Surprise rippled through Peter. He had to pull to a stop at the side of the road.

"If this is a prank call, you'd better pray I don't track you down," the voice warned.

Peter cleared his throat. "Marconi."

Silence answered him.

"It's Peter Myers."

"Myers?" Marconi's tone reflected the same shock Peter felt.

"Yeah."

Marconi whistled. "How did you get this number?"

"A friend let me know you have been calling a woman named Verna Timms every week for a while." Peter's mind raced. Why would someone like Marconi be calling Verna?

Marconi was part of an organized crime family. Peter's father had worked as their organization's lawyer for many years, but Peter had wanted nothing to do with them. If Verna was getting threatening calls from these dangerous criminals…

Peter waited, but Marconi said nothing. Finally, Peter was fed up. "Have you been threatening her?"

"No."

Peter snorted. "Why should I believe you?"

"Hold on. I'm just making sure I'm alone." Another few moments of silence went by before Marconi sighed over the line. "Verna Timms is my aunt. I call her every week to check up on her and make sure she's doing okay. So why are you checking up on her?"

How much should Peter tell him? If Verna fell as she claimed… but no. It made little sense. Someone was going after her, most likely Felix McNulty.

"Someone has been stealing her cats. She asked me to figure out who. Today, I stopped by her house to find her at the bottom of her basement steps. I think someone pushed her."

"Is she okay?" Marconi asked, the worry clear in his voice.

"Yes. She's got a mild concussion, but the doctors think she'll be okay. I'm just trying to figure out who did this." Peter cleared his throat. "I have to ask—do you know she used to work for the FBI?"

Marconi snorted. "Of course I do. But you don't need to know more than that."

"You ever heard of Felix McNulty?"

"Yes. Why?" Marconi's voice was wary again.

Peter explained the connection between McNulty and Verna. When he was done, Marconi growled aloud. He was clearly furious. Peter could hear it in his voice.

"You think McNulty hurt my aunt?" Marconi asked.

"I don't know," Peter said. "It's a possibility."

"I'll look into it. And Myers? Thanks for letting me know."

Marconi hung up, leaving Peter uncertain. Did he do the right thing by telling Marconi? It was too late to change now. He continued, finally getting to Verna's house.

Every light in the house was on. Someone was inside.

CHAPTER
NINE
TIMMS RESIDENCE

PETER PULLED the car up several houses away to avoid tipping off the intruder he was there. He called the police station, but the line was busy. Typical. Donnelly didn't have a proper reporting system. Whoever was in the house would be long gone before any of the inept police could get here, anyway.

There was only one thing for it. Peter searched his car for anything he could use as a defensive weapon but found nothing, not even a tire iron.

I will have to make myself a kit for my car if I keep doing this, he thought grimly as he got out of the car.

The blast of frigid wind hit him right in the face, stealing his breath. Ducking his head, Peter headed around the nearest house and crept through the backyards to Verna's house. The door leading to the catio was wide open.

Intruder at Verna's. Call Donnelly; Peter texted Jessica.

He turned the sound off his phone and slipped into the house. No cats came to greet him, but the loud sound of banging drawers and stomping feet came from above. Someone was on the upper floor, searching.

As Peter crept through the living room, he held in a gasp. The couches were cut open; vases and lamps were smashed on the floor. There were even holes punched into the walls. Whomever it was doing this wasn't just searching the house... they were ransacking the place.

Who would do this to a sweet old woman? Anger rose in Peter. Everything about this case made him angry. Verna was a good person who had dedicated her life to putting criminals away and only wanted to spend her golden years surrounded by the cats she so dearly loved.

She didn't deserve what was happening to her.

Peter headed up the stairs, sticking to the sides of the steps to keep them from creaking. When he reached the top, he pinpointed where the intruder was and charged. He smashed into the back of the intruder, and they rolled on the floor, fighting.

The intruder wore a hoodie and mask, with nylon stockings beneath the mask to hide their face. They punched Peter in the face. He tried to tackle back down but was distracted when he heard a plaintive meow from somewhere in the room. As his head turned, the intruder struck him again.

Darkness washed over his vision. The intruder threw him aside and raced away. By the time Peter returned to his feet and followed, they were gone.

He locked the doors and went back upstairs, following the meows. Soon, he found the cats stuffed into a small closet. They cried out and rubbed against his legs when he released them. Even the black cat, Hades, seemed happy to see him.

Peter counted them quickly. Eleven. That's how many Verna was supposed to have right now. Twelve would include the missing Persian, Persephone.

Peter pulled his phone from his pocket and sent a follow-up to Jessica. *Intruder gone. I'm staying the night here to clean up.*

Okay. I'll keep trying to get hold of Donnelly.

Thanks.

Peter sighed as he looked around. Well, better to start here. He grabbed a wastebasket off the floor and picked up the garbage. As he did so, he noticed a calendar on the floor. He picked it up, frowning at it.

Tomorrow's date was circled in red. Peter studied the calendar before putting it back on the wall where it began. He had a long night ahead of him.

CHAPTER
TEN
TIMMS RESIDENCE

IT WAS ALMOST noon when Peter was woken by a loud knock on the door. He groaned, covering his eyes to block out the sunlight. The last thing he wanted right now was to wake up.

The knock came again. Peter opened his eyes. For a moment, he forgot where he was. He seemed to have traveled back in time thirty or forty years. Something soft and warm curled up on his chest.

Right. He was at Verna's house, sleeping on the couch he'd pulled up from the basement. The old couch was a write-off, having been torn open so severely, but Verna had had a whole other entertainment setup in the basement.

More knocking, louder this time. The cats that had all piled up over him stirred. One of them purred right into his ear. He moved them aside as he sat up, yawning.

"I'll be there in a moment," he yelled.

The knocking stopped.

Peter searched for his shoes. He'd had a terribly long night. Donnelly had called him early morning to ask him about all the calls from Jessica but would not come out to check the scene himself.

Peter put his shoes back on and straightened his hair as he headed for the door. When he opened it, he found two officers from animal

THE FELINE CAPER   115

control on the other side, along with the woman sitting on the café patio glaring at Verna during his first meeting with her.

The woman's eyes widened in surprise. "Who are you?"

"Peter Myers," he said with a smile. "Verna Timms was hospitalized last night and asked me to watch her cats until she got out. Are you the inspection officers for the sanctuary?"

The two animal control officers glanced at each other. One of them cleared his throat. "Officer James here. I know nothing about a sanctuary, but we are here for an inspection."

Peter stepped back. "Please, come in."

The two officers came through. The woman, glaring at him, followed.

"And you're one of Verna's neighbors, aren't you?" Peter asked her politely.

The woman gave him a sneer and tossed her hair. "Mrs. Michelle Turner. What…"

As Peter led them into the living room, Michelle looked more shocked. Peter watched her closely.

Officer James scratched his head. "This isn't what we expected to find."

"Oh?" Peter picked up the sphinx cat and scratched its velvety skin. "What did you expect?"

"We were told we would confiscate neglected animals from a hoarding situation. But this place is amazing." Officer James looked distinctly impressed.

"They are neglected, and she is a hoarder," Michelle insisted. "This isn't what the house is supposed to look like. I mean, it's not what it looks like normally. He must have cleaned it up!"

"Verna has cleaners come in every day to help her," Peter said. "What did you expect? A house in utter disarray? Cat litter spread everywhere, perhaps? Or maybe you thought the catio screens would all be torn out?"

Michelle's face turned red as her hands tightened into fists at her sides.

Peter gestured around, turning his attention back to Officer James.

"There have been some problems with vandalism in the backyard, but I can assure you, there is no hoarding here. Verna runs an accredited cat sanctuary and fostering program. She works closely with our local vet."

Officer James scratched his head, looking bewildered.

"I don't care if she's an accredited sanctuary!" Michelle burst out. She stomped her foot in a childish display. "I'm a member of the neighborhood association, and I don't care who thought that crazy old lady should have permission to have so many cats."

"She has the licenses she needs; all these cats would be put down if she couldn't take them in."

"I don't care," Michelle screeched. "She has no right to keep them! She can't even keep track of them! Three of the little beasts escaped from her. They're the reason she fell down her stairs."

Ah, just as he had thought. Peter leveled a glare at the woman. "I never said she fell down the stairs."

"I... I..." Michelle's red face turned ashen.

Peter pulled his cell phone from his pocket. "You made a big mistake here, Mrs. Turner. And I think Captain Donnelly will be very interested in learning just how you knew Verna had fallen down the stairs. In fact, I'm sure Verna will identify you. I'm sure she already knows who pushed her down those stairs."

"How dare you?" Michelle rasped, her eyes widening in terror.

Peter smiled at her as he plugged in Donnelly's number. "I hope you didn't hurt those cats, Michelle. It'll be much worse for you if you did."

The woman trembled, then turned to bolt toward the door. As she raced down the hall, Hades suddenly leaped from a shelf near the ceiling. He landed hard in the square of her back, knocking her down. Peter hurried over and pulled her to her feet, the two animal control officers close behind him.

"Michelle Turner," Peter intoned as he clasped her arm. "I'm placing you under a citizen's arrest."

EPILOGUE
TIMMS RESIDENCE

WINTER LOOKED like it was going to arrive sooner rather than later. Peter sat on the porch of Verna's house, a mug of coffee in his hand. Verna had returned home only a few minutes ago, but it wasn't Jessica who brought her home as Peter had expected.

The door opened, and Marconi stepped out. He sank onto a chair close to Peter and leaned forward, resting his elbows against his knees.

"You and the vet lady will keep an eye on my aunt, right?" Marconi asked, a jaded look in his eyes.

"If you don't feel comfortable hanging around," Peter agreed.

Marconi eyed him but nodded. "I don't want to get her into trouble by consorting with a known criminal. I imagine you'll be telling your FBI contacts as soon as I return your phone."

Peter couldn't help but smile. When Marconi demanded he hand over his cell phone, Peter had obeyed without question. It wasn't as though the local police would do anything about it. Besides, if Marconi was so worried about his aunt, he should be allowed to make sure she was okay.

"The FBI has to know that you're her nephew already," Peter said, lifting his coffee. "And though I'd love to know how someone with such strong ties to organized crime got her position, I have a feeling that's above my clearance levels."

"Bet your boots it is," Marconi actually smiled. "Aunt Verna is in her room upstairs with the cats resting. Doctors say she should stay on bed rest for at least two days and to take her back into the hospital if she shows any signs of getting worse."

"We'll keep an eye on her," Peter promised.

Marconi nodded. He sighed as he leaned back in his chair. "I found McNulty and made sure he knew my aunt was off limits. He will not bother her. But he knew nothing about the cats."

"McNulty wasn't behind any of this," Peter explained.

"But you said—"

"I know what I said. I hadn't gotten all the puzzle pieces yet, though."

Marconi tilted his head and arched one eyebrow. "But you have it now?"

Peter sipped his coffee.

"Is the threat over?" Marconi demanded, sounding a little annoyed.

"Yes. I'll tell you what happened, but you have to promise not to take things into your own hands."

Marconi nodded tersely. "If the threat is over, I won't do anything."

"It was a member of the neighborhood association. Michelle Turner."

"That batty woman?" Marconi's eyes widened. "I know my aunt complained about her, but… why?"

Peter had to smile, even though the situation was not at all funny. It really was a horrible series of events. "Michelle Turner has been trying to get Verna's license as a sanctuary revoked for years. She thinks the catio is an eyesore that brings down property values."

Marconi rubbed his temples. "And I guess she doesn't care that these cats wouldn't survive without Aunt Verna?"

"No. She's a classic cat-hater." Peter drank another gulp of coffee. "It seems she got fed up with it all and thought if she could make Verna seem incompetent, she'd lose the cats entirely. So, she broke the locks on the front porch to steal Ares and later grabbed Hera from the yard."

"And Persephone? She never left the house," Marconi asked.

"She took out the window screen and lured Persephone into a carrying case with a can of tuna. All three cats were found in her house a mile away. Luckily, they're all still healthy. Her husband apparently thought she was rescuing strays and took good care of them."

Marconi rubbed the back of his neck. "I kept telling her she could lock her doors, but she insisted that Pine Grove was safe and she didn't need to."

"Michelle took advantage of it. When she learned I was looking into the cats' disappearances; she decided she needed to take it a step further. She pushed Verna down the stairs, figuring it would look like she tripped over her cats." Peter glared at the cloudy sky.

He didn't understand how anybody could think so highly of themselves that they would do any of this. Pushing an old woman down the stairs only proved that Michelle was a pathetic excuse for a person.

"She's in jail now," Peter continued. "Donnelly's bringing up charges of attempted murder."

Marconi let out a shuddering breath. He turned to Peter, his expression one of pure gratitude. "Thank you. You saved my aunt's life. I owe you one."

Peter waved a hand. "Yeah, well. I'm just glad she's going to be okay."

"I mean it. I owe you." Marconi stood. "And maybe next time I'm around this way, I'll find a way to pay you back. See you around?"

He held out his hand to Peter. Peter considered the man before him before accepting the hand. "Take care of yourself."

Marconi grinned and headed out. Peter drank his coffee, thinking about Jessica with the cats at the clinic, about Sam waiting for him at home, and this case solved. And he thought about how he never imagined one day he'd consider Marconi a friend.

"Funny old world," he mumbled to himself. "Hilarious."

The End

The Deadly Chili

A PINE GROVE MYSTERY

DAISY LANDISH

PROLOGUE
THE WOODS NEAR PINE GROVE

THE SUN'S heat beat against Eugene Morris' neck as he brushed aside a pile of soggy leaves. The first winter hits had disappeared suddenly, bringing New England into an odd, end-of-summer weather front. It surely meant winter would be unusual this year, but Eugene would deal with all that later.

The weather was now giving him an opportunity that his health had not. During prime time for mushroom foraging in the fall, he'd been laid up with a heavy cough that he had almost thought would kill him. But this second autumn had gotten the mushrooms growing once more.

His amber eyes glowed as he found the orange, fan-like ruffles of chicken of the woods. Eugene carefully harvested the delicate mushroom. He checked each one before wrapping it in waxed paper, then laid the packages gently in the base of the flat-bottomed wicker basket he always used in harvesting.

The basket had been a wedding present from his beloved Alexia fifty years ago. It was showing its age here and there, just as Eugene did. But he had repaired it when it failed, and this basket was still his best. A smile spread over his face as he stiffly got to his feet and moved on.

The smell of the damp forest and sun-soaked air lifted the old man's spirits. He would be happy if this were the last time he harvested mushrooms. It was a good harvest. He shuffled along, listening to crows talk to each other above him. He added to the tune with a cheerful whistle.

The day ended quicker than he wanted, but when he returned to his house, he lit a fire on the old wood stove. The cold of the night was driven out as he sorted out his forage.

Chicken of the woods. Lion's mane. Morels. Just what he needed.

"This will be my best year yet," Eugene said as he set his harvest before Alexia's smiling photo. He touched her lips as he settled into the old rocking chair. "You'll see. My best year."

CHAPTER
ONE

THE MAIN STREET CAFE

PETER MYERS FLIPPED the page of the Pine Grove newspaper, trying to give it his attention. Though it was yet another beautiful day outside, he sat inside the café today. The smell of eggs and bacon wafted out from the noisy kitchen.

There were other people with the newspaper today. He'd never seen so many people huddled around them, chatting animatedly. He shook his head as he flipped to the obituaries. It seemed morbid, but he hadn't reconnected with the people in Pine Grove and wanted to know who was still around and whom he could call on.

The café being as busy as it was, Peter wasn't sure how long it would be until he got the breakfast he ordered. He usually wasn't one to be antsy about waiting, but today he was.

Though it wasn't the food he was antsy about.

For the past few weeks, his budding relationship with the vet, Dr. Jessica Stern, had faded. Even though she was swamped these days, he couldn't help but feel that there was something more.

Maybe because he had doubted her convictions that Verna Timms, an elderly lady who was a good friend of Jessica's, really had been targeted when her cats disappeared. Jessica said she forgave him, as he had solved the case, but something just felt off since then.

First, it was missed dates, excuses not to see him, and finally, when he brought his dog, Sam, to the clinic for a checkup, Jessica didn't even see him; she had one of the other vets look at Sam. Peter wasn't sure what was happening, but he missed having her around. He hoped that she'd come to the café this morning. Maybe then he'd be able to talk with her, even if it was only to walk her to her office.

Not that he was stalking her, of course. He often came to the café himself after his morning run, just as Jessica often stopped for coffee before her morning shift. This was the first time in a while he'd come in, and that was because he didn't want Jessica to think he was stalking her.

If he could 'accidentally' bump into her, he might be able to find out what was happening. Have a pleasant chat, maybe invite her to dinner or a movie. Or he could even volunteer to bring her lunch to the clinic since she was so busy.

"I don't enter anymore," a middle-aged man snorted from a table next to Peter. "Eugene Morris wins it every year. The man's got some sort of magic recipe."

Peter glanced up to find the man sitting next to two bored-looking teenagers, his face buried in the newspaper while they both played on their phones.

He straightened when the door to the café opened, and a familiar face walked in. Marconi, a gangster from the city—well, Peter was pretty sure he was still a gangster. What was he doing here?

Marconi's gaze swept the café as he headed toward the counter. It lingered briefly on Peter, and he inclined his head.

Their last meeting was friendly enough. Peter hesitated before he nodded back. He had thought Marconi was too noticeable for a small town like Pine Grove. Had something happened with Verna? The friendly old woman was Marconi's aunt.

Still, Peter carefully watched Marconi as the man stopped at the counter.

"Order for Timms," Marconi grunted, turning slightly so he could still survey the café, which was expected from a man who was used to watching his back constantly.

The harried server behind the counter sorted through receipts before nodding. "Ah, yes! That's pancakes, eggs, sausages, bacon, hash browns—"

"Yes," Marconi interrupted, leaning against the counter.

"Right. So let me just…." The server turned to a stack of Styrofoam takeout containers. She hurriedly packed them in a bag while Marconi glanced idly over the notice board.

He straightened suddenly, touching one notice as he read it to himself. Peter frowned at what had caught Marconi's interest so much. He was so involved in the notice that when the server handed over two bags of takeout, she had to clear her throat and call out to him twice.

Marconi grabbed the bags, glanced at Peter once more, and headed out.

Curiosity swept over Peter. He set his newspaper aside and stood, stretching. Then, trying to appear casual, he headed over to look at the bulletin board. He quickly found the advert that Marconi was so interested in. Peter's brow furrowed as he read it.

Fortieth Annual Chili Cookoff

The date was listed, along with a website, to get more information and where you could go to register—a chili cookoff. Peter had heard about this for a while, but why was Marconi so interested in it?

The server behind the counter cleared her throat. "May I help you?"

"Oh, I was just looking at this while I waited for my breakfast," Peter said, smiling at her.

Despite his attempts at being reassuring, the poor girl paled. "Oh, I'm so sorry! I'll check with the cook—"

"No, no, don't worry about it." Peter shook his head, regretting that he had startled her. "I'm not in any rush; I was just curious about the chili cookoff. Do you know anything about it?"

The server, whose nametag read Daphne, nodded as she shifted from foot to foot. She was young, possibly as young as sixteen, and as Peter hadn't seen her here before, he thought she must be a new worker. The poor girl looked terrified.

"Everyone gets involved in the cookoff," she explained, glancing at the advert. "It's a huge deal. We have a chili parade, and then the chili mayor is elected from the best costumes in the parade, and they preside over the cookoff. The contestants spend all day cooking, and then the judges decide who's best."

"I see."

Daphne leaned over the counter. "There are different prizes for the different areas. I heard this year for the teams; it's a trip for two to the Bahamas. I'd love to enter. But I don't know how to make chili. Eugene Morris is teaming up with Captain Donnelly anyway... they'll win for sure. Mr. Morris always wins."

"Thanks," Peter mumbled.

But he wasn't thinking about Morris and Donnelly. Instead, his mind swirled around the trip for two to the Bahamas. And wondered if Jessica would like to take part in a cooking competition.

CHAPTER
TWO
THE MYERS' RESIDENCE

JESSICA RAN a hand through her hair, grimacing as she did so. The drastic change in weather affected the staff at the clinic and their animal patients. She was down two vet techs and had been slammed with sick animals. In a small town like this, most of her patients didn't come to the clinic—they were the large farm animals in the surrounding rural areas.

She had had so many emergency calls this past week that she barely spent time in town. A nice, hot bath was just what the doctor ordered...

But she knew as soon as she got home, she was going to be so exhausted that all she'd want to do was a quick shower before falling into bed.

Pulling to a stop outside Peter's house, she grabbed her travel bag and slipped from her Jeep Cherokee. Peter had left her a text message and a voicemail asking if she could stop by tonight, which sounded urgent. She just hoped that nothing was wrong with Sam.

Hurrying to the door, she rang the bell.

A few minutes later, Peter opened up. His eyes widened in surprise before a pleased smile broke over his face.

"Jessica. I'm glad you came. I wasn't expecting you."

"But I sent you a message saying I'd come over after work," Jessica protested.

Peter stepped aside and gestured her inside. He pulled his phone from his pocket as he shut the door.

"I didn't get it," he said. "Maybe the reception can be spotty here."

A wave of dread washed over Jessica. She set her bag down and pulled out her phone; it took less than a minute to realize that while she had typed up a return message to Peter, she had never sent it. She groaned as she rubbed her temples.

"Sorry. I've just been so frazzled all day." Jessica was happy to see Sam trot into the hallway, his tail wagging. From a glance, she saw his coat looked good, his eyes were bright, and he looked good.

"It's fine. I wasn't expecting you," Peter said.

Jessica knelt to pet Sam. "How are you, boy? Do you need a vet visit?"

"No," Peter said quickly. "Sorry, I didn't mean to make you think Sam was sick. I actually was hoping we could have dinner, maybe watch a movie afterward?"

Jessica straightened. She could smell a spicy, meaty dish cooking, and her stomach rumbled.

"Would you have enough for two, even though you weren't expecting me?" she asked, a little embarrassed.

Peter grinned. "You're in luck. I was planning on bringing some of it to the vet clinic tomorrow. Come on in and take a load off your feet."

Even though she always kept a few changes of clothes in the jeep, she didn't think it would be appropriate to ask Peter if she could use his shower. It would be awkward, she decided, especially as she wasn't exactly sure where their relationship was at.

Jessica liked Peter. She had from the first time he brought Sam into her clinic. But he was a lawyer; he'd worked with the FBI for years and made a comfortable living for himself so that he could retire even though he was only in his fifties. Yeah, he had come back to Pine Grove, but Jessica still couldn't help but feel that one day he'd tire of this place.

Right now, though, she wasn't in the headspace to have that discussion. She put it from her mind as she followed him into the kitchen.

"It smells delicious," she said as she headed for the cupboards, intent on setting the table.

Peter stepped in front of her and put his hands on her shoulders. "You look exhausted. Sit down. I'll serve up dinner. I hope you like chili."

Jessica's mouth watered. "Chili," she said, "is the greatest gift God gave humanity. I don't care what anybody else says."

Peter laughed as he pulled two bowls from the cupboard and dished it up. "I found an old recipe from my mom that she got from her grandmother. I've been thinking about this chili cookoff. Do you think you'd be interested in taking part? I know it's a lot of pressure when you're already busy."

Jessica's face split into a grin. Was she interested? She fought the urge to pump her fist. "Oh, I'm interested. I have the perfect recipe. It's delicious. Savory, with a fresh snap of heat to it. The only problem is that it takes two chefs to prepare everything."

"Oh?" Peter handed her a bowl and spoon. "And here I thought I would have to use my amazing chili recipe to sway you to my side."

Jessica scooped out a spoonful and sniffed it. Kidney beans, ground beef, molasses, chili, cumin, coriander, garlic, and bell peppers. The scents were all there. It was still hot, so she blew on it to cool it.

"I have been looking for a partner to help me take on Eugene Morris for *years*," Jessica said, gleaming. She tasted the chili. The balance of flavor was full and hearty. Perfect. "I've almost given up."

"The theme this is 'Chili Vacanti,'" Peter said. "A play on 'chill vacation,' so it seems. The grand prize is a trip for two to the Bahamas."

Jessica had never been to the Bahamas. The furthest from New England she had been was when she went to Cornell University to study as a veterinarian. That was in Ithaca, New York. A free trip to a place as tropical as the Bahamas? And with someone like Peter?

Maybe then we can figure out what this is between us, she thought.

Jessica grinned in response to Peter's hopeful look. "Just be warned, Peter Myers. I am a very competitive person."

Peter laughed and lifted his spoon as though toasting. "Then this competition will be ours!"

CHAPTER
THREE

IN THE WOODS NEAR THE MYERS' RESIDENCE

THE PALE SUNLIGHT trickled in through the treetops, casting an almost ghostly glow to the forest, even though it was brightly lit. Peter's breath was barely visible, but the crisp air left him wishing he had pulled on gloves before leaving the house.

Meanwhile, Sam was having a blast. He kicked up leaves and chased after them. Twice he'd picked up a stick and brought it back to Peter. Not to play fetch but so that Peter could bring it home. He was a funny dog like that.

When Peter started his daily jogs along the deer path in the woods near his place, he was concerned about letting Sam off the leash. He shouldn't have been worried. Sam was the sort of dog that liked to be with people. In fact, if he found something interesting and Peter hid from him, he'd start whining and barking. All it took was a single reminder for Peter to call him back to his side.

It probably had to do with the fact that Sam was abandoned in these woods.

"But you're with me now, aren't you, boy?" Peter asked Sam.

Sam wagged his tail. "Woof!" he said, then bounded after a particular leaf. When he caught it, he proudly brought it back to Peter.

They were just about to turn back home when Sam suddenly stiffened. The hairs on his neck bristled, and he pressed close to Peter's legs, growling.

"What is it?" Peter asked, peering through the trees.

"Ruff!" Sam barked.

Peter caught sight of something moving. He tensed, but it soon became apparent it wasn't a bear or lynx but a human. "Hello?" he called.

A brief pause stilled the forest before someone called back, "Is someone there?"

"Peter Myers," Peter answered, moving cautiously forward. Sam trembled against his leg but stayed with him.

Soon, he could see the other person clearly. He has seen the old man around town. It only took a moment for Peter to place him. It was Eugene Morris, the man everyone kept talking about. Peter remembered him from when he grew up in Pine Grove. He was one of Myers' closest neighbors.

"Peter!" Eugene said, a genuine smile breaking over his face. He carried a patched-up wicker basket on his arm, a dark plaid coat, too big for him, buttoned up to his neck.

Sam relaxed and bounded forward. "Woof!"

Eugene looked at him and laughed. "If it isn't Mr. Shaggy. Hi, boy."

He reached out a hand, allowing Sam to sniff it before patting his head.

"How do you know, Sam?" Peter asked in surprise.

"Is he your dog?" Eugene asked.

Peter laughed. "He is now. I found him in the forest, and he just adopted me."

Eugene nodded as he reached into his pocket to pull out a dog biscuit. "I'm glad he found you. I've seen this handsome fella around, but I could never get close enough to take him to the vet in town. He looks so much healthier now. I'd feed him when I could, but I've got a bunch of coyotes that always try to attack him when he came round."

Peter smiled at his dog. He was glad to have Sam, too. "He's a wonderful dog. I wish I knew who had abandoned him in the first place."

Eugene nodded once. "You and me both."

This was a bit of a depressing topic, so Peter cleared his throat. "So, I hear around town that you're the reigning chili cookoff champ."

"Yup." Eugene lifted his basket. "And I'm lucky that the weather has changed enough for me to get my secret weapon."

"Mind if I take a look?" Peter asked, curious. What could he be getting out here in the forest for something like that?

Eugene pulled back a plaid covering from the basket and tenderly lifted out a white, stringy-looking mushroom. "I forage them myself every year. Nothing beats the taste of a wild mushroom. Here, take a sniff."

Peter accepted the proffered fungus and held it to his nose. It smelled earthy, with that delicate aroma he always associated with mushrooms. "I've never seen one like this before."

"That's because you have never foraged, my boy." Eugene placed the mushroom in his basket. "You'll find that people around here try to put a unique spin on chili. Your mother, I believe, had a delicious, sweet chili recipe. Molasses and honey with something I could never quite put my finger on. Before she passed, rest her soul, she was a strong contender against me."

Peter smiled back. "Well, I hope I live up to her name, then. I'm entering the competition with Jessica Stern."

The old man smiled widely. "Oh, good! Nothing like cooking with a… friend. Well, I'd best be off."

"As should I," Peter agreed.

They shook hands in parting and headed in opposite directions. Peter hummed as he headed toward his house. Secret weapon, huh? He hoped his secret weapon—Jessica's sheer determination to win—would serve him as well as foraged mushrooms.

CHAPTER FOUR

MAIN STREET GROCERS, PINE GROVE

PETER COULDN'T HELP but grin at Jessica's enthusiasm as she compared the two types of cheese in her hands. Based on how she acted, one might think this chili cookoff was a matter of national security. Despite having bought most of the ingredients they needed for Jessica's perfect chili recipe, they also had plenty of ingredients they didn't need.

"So that nobody can spy in our basket and figure out the secret ingredient," Jessica explained to him as she set one cheese back and put the other in the basket. She glanced around and lowered her voice, "Besides, none of this is going to waste. We can donate what we don't use to the food bank."

"You're the boss," Peter replied, keeping his voice low.

Jessica grinned at him and consulted her list. "All right. Let's get some anchovies and black beans now."

"Anchovies. That would be a surprise in chili, wouldn't it?"

Jessica elbowed him in the ribs. "Shhh! You'll give it away."

Peter pulled the imaginary zipper across his lips and pretended to lock them. Jessica rolled her eyes, though her grin was still firmly in place. Peter thought she was enjoying herself and was glad. Now that they were spending more time with each other, she had told him about everything happening at the clinic—he couldn't imagine how exhausting it must be.

They turned down the aisle with canned fish when a voice called behind them.

"Myers!"

Peter turned. He had to fight off his surprise when he saw the man waving his hand. It was Marconi. What was he still doing in Pine Grove?

"Myers," Marconi repeated as he pushed a grocery cart closer. He grinned. "How are you doing?"

"Fine," Peter kept his tone calm. Beside him, Jessica cleared her throat. Oh, no. She had to wonder who this man was and how Peter knew him. But Marconi was a gangster and putting him in close contact with Jessica seemed like a bad idea.

Not that Peter would ever think about a gangster with a shopping cart full of beans, sugar, and cat food.

"Pardon me," Marconi said, holding his hand out to Jessica. "I'm Martin Timms. Peter and I know each other from out in the city. He calls me Marconi, don't you?"

Peter forced a smile, scrambling to produce a reason he'd do that. "Actually, it started with me calling him Marconi because every time I saw him, he was waiting for Mac 'n' Cheese. It just developed from there."

Marconi laughed as though he was enjoying an old story between friends.

"Timms," Jessica repeated as she shook his hand. "Of course. Verna told me her nephew was going to come to stay with her. How is she doing?"

Peter's brow furrowed. "Has something happened?"

"She needed minor surgery," Marconi replied with a wave of his hand. "I'm sticking around and helping her out while she recovers. It's nothing serious, but Aunt Verna likes the attention."

But as he spoke, Marconi glanced at Peter again. There was something in his eyes. A warning, perhaps? Peter tried to keep his expression smooth. Marconi might have a ready explanation, but it didn't seem to be the entire story.

"Are you entering the cookoff, too?" Jessica asked, peering into Marconi's cart.

Marconi pulled it aside and stepped in front of it, trying to hide the ingredients. "Not me, personally. I have a friend who decided to join, and I'm helping him prepare. I see you picked up some jalapeno peppers for yours."

"Of course," Jessica said, blocking their cart as she craned her neck to look around Marconi.

Peter sighed. Her competitive streak was acting up again. She was trying to figure out what Marconi's secret ingredient was. Peter pushed their cart a little further back.

"It was good seeing you," he quickly said, wanting to break this awkward encounter. "I guess we'll meet again at the cookoff."

Marconi touched his forehead in a mock salute.

Jessica gathered a can of anchovies and then some salmon and tuna. She hummed thoughtfully. "Did you see he had some sweet potato? I wonder if he's putting it in his chili. He seems like a nice person."

"Yeah. He's a real prince." Peter winced at the sarcasm in his voice. He shrugged apologetically at Jessica as she gave him a startled glance. "I'm sure he matured a lot since my college days."

Jessica elbowed him in the ribs. "I should hope you have as well. 'Macaroni' indeed."

Peter kept an eye out for the mobster as they finished up their shopping. As Jessica got in line for the checkout, he spied Marconi again. He hesitated, not wanting to bring more attention to the two of them—but there had to be more than helping Verna and this cookoff getting Marconi here.

He excused himself and headed over to the gangster.

"Hope I didn't ruin your date," Marconi said idly as he chose the best head of lettuce for his cart.

"What are you doing here, Marconi?" Peter asked in a hiss.

Marconi looked up with an arched brow. "I'm looking after my aunt, of course."

Peter narrowed his eyes. "We both know that's not true. You would not stay here after she was pushed down those stairs because you stood out too much in a small town like this. So why now?"

Marconi grabbed a bunch of cilantro. "Looking after my aunt. You really should be worried about yourself, Myers. Watch your own back instead of mine, yeah?"

Peter bristled at the veiled threat. "And here I thought we were friends."

"We are friends. Or close enough." Marconi pushed his cart, edging past Peter. "That's why I'm giving you the warning."

CHAPTER
FIVE
THE TIMMS' RESIDENCE

MARCONI ROLLED his shoulders as he finished putting his groceries away, then grabbed a can of soup to heat up. He usually wouldn't be doing this sort of thing, but having his crew watch his aunt's twelve cats while they lay low here in Pine Grove was already getting on their nerves.

They knew, though, if any of them so much as looked at one of these cats wrong, they'd end up gutted. Marconi didn't enjoy bringing the gangsters around here. That's why he had his aunt stay in the city for a couple of weeks and claimed she had surgery to explain why she wasn't around. He didn't want his men to think they could use her to get to him if there were a traitor in their midst.

That and the fact she was a former FBI agent. Marconi didn't know how she'd gotten the position when her brother and nephew were in the mafia, and he didn't want to know. Just like she didn't want to know what he was up to these days.

As soon as Marconi opened the can of soup, a flurry of meows and tiny pattering feet charged into the kitchen. A graceful cat leaped onto the counter and purred as she rubbed against his arm.

"No, Aphrodite," he said sharply, pushing her off the counter again. "I've fed all of you this morning. You don't need more."

Aphrodite wound around his legs and let out a pitiful cry.

Marconi rolled his eyes. He was packing on the weight around his middle, making him look even shorter than he was because his aunt insisted that he wasn't eating enough. But Heaven forbid he deviated from the strict feeding schedule she left for her kitties.

"Yo, Marconi." Tall and thin Russo, his thick hair pulled into a side part which made him look younger, sidled into the kitchen. He held the sphinx cat in his arms, stretching it idly behind the ears as it snuggled into his neck. "When are we going to make our move? The boys and I have been talking. We've got nothing but time on our hands and—"

"You know the plan," Marconi replied sharply.

Russo's jaw snapped shut.

Marconi dumped his canned soup into a pot and put it on the stove to heat. "We do nothing until the contest. It's the key. If you're eager for something to do, you can change the litter boxes."

Russo made a face. "I did that this morning," he complained.

"Then go watch some TV. The contest," Marconi repeated. "And not before."

CHAPTER
SIX

PINE GROVE CENTENNIAL PARK,
10 A.M.

PETER CLUTCHED his phone in one hand as he and Jessica hurried down the line to the far end, searching for their cooking station. Jessica pulled her coat around her, her cheeks bright with anticipation and the cold. They were looking forward to getting into the half-tent station with all their cooking gear.

"What did Rina want?" Jessica asked as she adjusted the straps of her satchel.

Peter glanced at his phone before he had to catch the cooler with both hands. He and Jessica carried it between them, and he had stumbled.

"Rina and Matt both wanted to wish me luck," Peter explained, keeping his eyes on the path so as not to trip them up again.

Jessica made a noise of approval. "That was really sweet of them. Tell them I said thanks."

"Will do."

Peter smiled. He hadn't officially introduced his two children to Jessica yet. It was still a little too soon—not just because their relationship was still in the early stages, but because Rina and Matt were still getting used to the divorce. They weren't little kids, but it didn't matter what age you were. It hurt when parents broke up… even if it was for the best.

"Hurry," Jessica squealed. "We have ten minutes to set up!"

He picked up his pace, and they were soon at their station. The cookoff was taking place in Centennial Park, but with another cold turn in the weather, the stations were closed on three sides, all facing against the wind.

As Peter started putting out their supplies, he glanced up the line. He fumbled with a jar of chili spice, and Jessica had to catch it before it hit the ground.

"Careful!" she said.

Peter tried to concentrate on his work. He tried to ignore that their next-door competitor was Marconi, with two of his henchmen. Marconi stood outside the station, talking in a low voice with one of his men. Further up the line were more men with a look about them that Peter had seen all too well. Though they tried to blend in, he'd seen their faces when he was prosecuting various gangsters for the FBI.

His shoulders were tense, and his jaw clenched. He tried to ignore them as he helped Jessica lay out their supplies in the proper order. She hurried to fill their big stock pot with broth as the Chili Mayor started his welcoming speech.

Clearly, Marconi was weighing the contest heavily in his favor, but Peter couldn't bring it up without proof that they were all connected. Maybe he could get Tiff to send out a few people. But what was Marconi after? What could he possibly want from running a scam on a small-town chili cookoff?

"Peter, we forgot the beans!" Jessica grabbed his arm, her eyes wide with panic.

"I'll get them," he quickly volunteered.

He raced back toward the parking lot. Five minutes left. Anything not at their station then wasn't allowed to be used. His eyes skimmed the other stations as he passed them.

Leah, the queen of high school from when Peter was a teen, stood in one station. Her lanky hair was a mess around her head, and the skin-tight bodysuit was terribly unflattering. She had a cigarette in her hand—was her secret ingredient ash? She argued with her partner, who was waving a hairnet at her.

Next was Eugene Morris, his station immaculate as he stood at the entrance, scowling as he glared toward the parking lot. Right, he was supposed to be partnered with Captain Donnelly. It appeared his partner was late.

Peter took a moment to find Tiff's number in the parking lot and called her. He grabbed the beans out of the car and pinched the phone to his ear, ensuring nothing else was left behind.

"Pick up," he hissed. Three minutes. "Pick up!"

Only the beans were missing. He locked the car and raced back toward his station. He bit back an angry grunt as Tiff's phone went to voicemail. Usually, she was quick to pick up... just his luck that she wouldn't answer this time.

He gave a quick rundown of the contest in a low voice as he passed the other cooking stations. "See if you can find out what's happening. Maybe he's got a bet on the outcome, or they're running something. I don't know."

He hung up as he slid into the station, where Jessica finished putting everything out. He passed her the beans, and she dumped them into a pot just as the Cookout Mayer announced it open. Peter panted as he leaned against the stove.

"Just in time," he heard a boastful voice crow.

Peter leaned out to see that Captain Donnelly had joined Eugene. Eugene shoved an apron into his chest.

"Peter," Jessica said.

"Yeah, I'm here," Peter answered. He quickly got back into the station to prepare for the cookoff.

He had to admit he was more than distracted... and angry at himself. He should have been more suspicious when he saw Marconi shopping. Of course, it would not be as innocent as helping a friend out. The only question was, what was this really about?

CHAPTER
SEVEN

PINE GROVE CENTENNIAL PARK,
11:50 A.M.

A HUM of excitement filled the park. While the main path was sectioned off for the cookoff, there were plenty of things to entertain the people while the chilis were prepared—a bouncy castle for little ones, various kiosks selling trinkets, and of course, the food. Everyone was excited about sharing in the chili at the end, but in the meantime, stomachs rumbled.

Jessica loved it. Everything about the cookoff was fantastic. The scent of food and spices invigorated her.

"Peter, do you think these onions are caramelized enough?" she asked as she flitted from one pan to the next, ensuring everything was cooking properly.

He looked over at her, jumping slightly as though he'd forgotten where they were. "What?"

Jessica frowned at him, irritated. She had never thought of Peter Myers as a flake before, yet he kept getting distracted. He wasn't even halfway finished dicing the tomatoes yet.

"What is wrong with you?" she groused. Her competitive streak was shining through. "You're not acting like yourself. Is the pressure getting to you?"

She couldn't leave the stove. These dishes needed constant attention; it was why just one person couldn't make the chili. The prep work had to be done on time, but she couldn't take her eyes off the pots.

"No," Peter said. He renewed dicing the tomatoes. "I was just distracted by Marconi's man over there. Have you seen his knife skills?"

Jessica glanced at their nearest competitor. The one man didn't seem to do much other than peeling a few vegetables while the other was hard at work. It was impressive how much he'd gotten done already.

She turned her attention back to her work. "Doesn't matter. You're behind because you got distracted. So don't be distracted; we need to catch up."

The onions could use a little more time to caramelize at that. She turned the heat a little lower and checked the beans medley. They weren't getting cooked fast enough. She turned up the heat, then moved to the sauce base.

"Hurry with the tomatoes; I need them," she called over her shoulder.

"Jess—"

Peter was interrupted by a blood-curdling shriek. Jessica leaped from the station at once, looking to see what had happened. Up the line, Eugene Morris stumbled from his station, clutching his stomach with one hand. A spoon with chili sauce still on it was clutched in his other hand. He dropped like a puppet with its strings cut.

"Peter, call the paramedics," Jessica yelled over her shoulder as she ran to help Eugene.

She dropped to her knees beside him as he panted, a strange foam building at the corners of his lips. Jessica's heart seized. She'd seen enough dogs and cats come in with these symptoms to know what it was.

PETER REACHED Jessica's shoulder as he spoke with the paramedics. The judges and the Chili Mayor gathered around, and Peter handed his phone off to the mayor to keep on the line while he bent down next to Jessica.

"What can I do?" he asked tersely.

"Help me get him to his side. You," she pointed at another chef. "Bring me latex gloves, stat!"

The woman blinked in surprise but hurried back to her station. Peter dropped to his knees next to Jessica and helped to roll Eugene to his side. When the chef returned with the gloves, Jessica snapped one onto her hand and pried Eugene's mouth open. His skin was clammy, and he wasn't responding to anything.

Jessica stuck her finger down his throat.

Peter understood instantly. He looked up to see Captain Donnelly stirring their chili sauce with a frown. He lifted the spoon toward his lips—

Peter lunged, knocking the police captain backward. What a stupid way to see if something was wrong with it! Donnelly collapsed into the side of his station, and Peter reached to knock the spoon from his hand.

"What's the matter with you?" Donnelly yelled, shoving Peter.

"You don't stick something in your mouth that made your partner collapse," Peter seethed at the captain. Behind them, Eugene gagged.

Donnelly pushed Peter off and scrambled to his feet. "Eugene has a nervous stomach. He's old and was just sick a couple of weeks ago. He probably was pushing himself too hard."

Peter glared at the captain. Out of all the times for the man to be incompetent, now wasn't the time. "Are you so sure, Captain? Maybe if you paid attention to what is happening, you'd see Jessica inducing vomit."

Donnelly looked over Peter's shoulder. By the sounds coming from Eugene, Peter knew Jessica was correct.

"I need a Ziploc bag. Something to take a sample of for the paramedics," she said.

Donnelly blustered wordlessly, making confused noises.

Peter stepped closer to him and lowered his voice. "Eugene has won this competition for years. And I'm seeing many people who look like they'd do anything to win this contest."

Donnelly's jaw dropped as his eyes widened. "What are you saying, Myers? That Eugene was poisoned?"

CHAPTER
EIGHT

PINE GROVE CENTENNIAL PARK,
12:15 P.M.

DONNELLY PUT his hands on his hips and narrowed his eyes at Peter. "You're the one who knew he was poisoned. As far as I'm concerned, he who smelt it dealt it."

Peter shook his head in annoyance. "That's about passing gas, Donnelly. Besides, I'm not the one who first recognized it as poison; Jessica is. You know, the trained veterinarian?" he added.

"Lots of animals are brought in with similar symptoms during the mushroom season," Jessica said. She was over at the chili sauce, looking through it.

After the paramedics arrived to take Eugene to the hospital, Captain Donnelly ordered the park festivities to continue, except that his deputies interrogate people and not let anyone leave. The cookout was at a standstill, though, as the other chefs were the prime suspects.

"The mushrooms he used must be poisonous," Leah complained as she stood beside her partner, tapping her foot impatiently. "There's nothing to investigate."

Peter ignored her. Eugene was far too precise in his foraging to pick anything poisonous.

Jessica picked a small piece of mushroom out of the chili sauce. She let out a low whistle as she held it up. "I think this is it. It doesn't look like any mushrooms Eugene normally puts in his sauce."

"Can you remember all the mushrooms you and Eugene practiced with?" Peter asked Donnelly.

Donnelly snorted. "How am I supposed to know that? Eugene was the mycologist."

More proof he wouldn't have accidentally poisoned himself. Peter joined Jessica, his brow furrowed in worry. What was going on here?

"Eugene might have decided that his mushroom recipe was getting old; he's used the same one for years," Donnelly continued. "Maybe he added in something new last minute. I was late, after all."

"See?" Leah called. Her brash voice grated on Peter's nerves. "It's that old man's fault. Let's just continue the contest. My chili's going to burn if this continues. So, let's just go; we don't have to stop just because some stupid old man mixed up his ingredients."

Peter turned to her, annoyed and disgusted with her. "Eugene could die from this. With his experience and training, he wouldn't have made such a careless mistake."

"I'm inclined to believe he would," Donnelly interrupted.

Peter clenched his jaw so tight it hurt.

Luckily, Jessica stepped into the space between him and Donnelly. "Why would you say that? Eugene—"

"Is old," Donnelly said.

"He's not that old," Jessica protested.

Donnelly shrugged. "The mind does strange things. He hasn't been the same since his wife, God rest her soul, passed away. Maybe he did it on purpose. Maybe he's committing suicide."

Peter gently touched Jessica's wrist. "You're a fool, Donnelly."

"And you're causing a fuss over nothing," Donnelly huffed. "I'm the police Captain here, Myers. Don't forget it. We continue the competition. Everyone, get back to your stations."

Peter was going to argue, but Jessica caught his hand in hers. "If we keep quiet, maybe we'll be able to investigate on the down low," she mumbled.

It was better than anything Donnelly was going to offer. Even though Peter didn't like it, he still nodded. As he and Jessica returned to their station, though, he tensed again. Marconi's man hadn't left his station, still hard at work. Marconi stood to one side of the stove, looking on innocently.

Peter opened his mouth as they passed but shut it again. He would not put a target on Jessica's back by making her aware that Marconi wasn't who he said he was. This business was between the two of them—Jessica would not get caught in the crossfire, not if Peter had anything to say about it.

CHAPTER
NINE

THE BEANS WERE salvageable for Peter and Jessica's chili, but the sauce and everything else Jessica had been cooking were ruined. Peter kept a close eye on the other contestants as he stood outside the station, working at the stove while Jessica tried to pull something out of what they had left.

She didn't seem to be as interested in winning anymore. The gusto with which she had been working before was gone entirely. In its stead was a nervousness that held sway over the entire park. The number of people had halved since Eugene was taken away.

Peter breathed out a breath full of anxious energy. He wasn't about to call it quits himself, even though he had no interest in making chili anymore. It would be another three and a half hours before the judging began—the cookoff was an all-day event.

At Eugene's old station, loud mutterings and curses came from Donnelly as he was trying to make a new batch of chili without his partner or Eugene's secret weapon. For as incompetent as the man was as a police captain, he was surprisingly inventive with cooking.

Jessica stepped up to the stock pot and tipped in some excess peelings. "Seeing anything interesting?"

"Donnelly is fuming. I don't think he's the one that poisoned Eugene. If anything, he was riding Eugene's coattails."

"What about Leah?" Jessica asked. "She didn't seem at all concerned."

Peter hummed, not sure how to continue. He wasn't worried about Leah. She had peaked in high school and didn't have the means to pull something like this off. No, Peter was still focused on Marconi's men. The various stations with his mobsters were cooking as though nothing had happened.

The cook in the station next to Peter and Jessica tasted his chili and kissed the air. "Voila! That is what you call chili," he boasted.

Peter frowned at the man. He seemed far too confident. Even the reigning champion had been nervous before all of this started. What made this man think that he was going to beat everyone else?

"Do you know that guy?" Peter asked, nodding toward the cook.

Jessica glanced over at him and shook her head. "He looks familiar, but I can't place him. The café?"

"No, the café cook is over there with Leah," Peter gestured. He had just recognized her partner.

"Don't know then," Jessica said and retreated into the station.

Peter continued to stir the cooking ingredients, pondering the situation. He didn't believe that Eugene would have put a poisonous mushroom in his chili, which means someone else did. Was it Marconi? Was that why he was in Pine Grove, to win this contest?

But why? Why poison a harmless old man? Why go to these lengths? If Marconi wanted to go to the Bahamas for any reason, he had to have better means of planning his trip than to win a chili contest.

What is going on here? Peter wondered.

A bang and pop came from Leah's station. A flame ball burst from the stove. Her partner yelled and dove for the ground while Leah screamed. Jessica started forward, but Peter held out an arm, stopping her.

"Stay here," he told her. "Make sure nobody goes near our ingredients or the equipment."

Leah started shouting, a mix of fear and anger in her voice. "You idiot! What did you do? You always turn off the propane first!"

Her partner, now smothering the flames with a wet towel, snapped back. "I didn't do anything. I told you, you're useless at cooking. You should have just let me—"

"I'm useless?" Leah screamed.

Jessica once more tried to pass Peter, but he turned to her and shook his head. "We can't leave this stuff unguarded."

"Unguarded?" Jessica repeated, searching his gaze. "What do you mean? What's going on?"

Peter took a deep breath. It wasn't safe for her not to know now. "Sabotage."

CHAPTER
TEN

PINE GROVE CENTENNIAL PARK,
4:45 P.M.

CAPTAIN DONNELLY GLARED AT PETER. "I'm tired of arguing with you about this, Myers."

"You're only arguing with me because you can't see what's happening here," Peter responded.

"Oh, you think that you suddenly know everything just because you figured out a few domestic problems in this town?" Donnelly pointed a sauce-stained spoon at him. "Get back to your cooking station. I'll arrest you if you interrupt me again with these wild theories."

After over three hours of trying to convince the captain to call off the cookout for the participants' safety, Peter finally had to admit defeat. He'd done his best to figure out what was happening here, but he was no closer to it than when he started.

Annoyed and worried, Peter returned to where Jessica was cooking. Her hair was frizzy from the humidity of cooking, and her eyes were rimmed with red. She'd been crying.

Peter's heart lurched. He hurried forward to take his part in the cooking. "Hey, I'm sorry. Have you heard anything about Eugene?"

"No. It's the onions."

Peter knew that wasn't true. Jessica had finished cutting the onions hours ago. He sighed miserably. "I'm sorry."

"Don't say sorry. Just tell me what's going on here." She gave him a piercing look.

"I don't know," Peter hedged.

"You know more than what you're telling me."

Peter glanced at Marconi. He was over in the activities section of the park, eating a corn dog. An amused smile was on his face, and Peter knew it wasn't because someone had just told him a good joke. His hackles raised. He had half a mind to go over there and demand answers...

Not that it would do much good.

Peter pulled his phone from his pocket and called Tiff.

"Peter," Jessica complained.

"Sorry," he muttered, but Tiff answered, and he took a few steps away from the station. "Tiff, have you learned anything?"

"Not really," Tiff replied sadly.

Jessica made a noise in her throat. "Oh, so you're going to keep me in the dark but call another woman?"

Peter took another few steps and lowered his voice. "Is the contest a front for the mob?"

"No. It's been an annual tradition for what seems like forever in Pine Grove," Tiff replied. "I can't imagine anyone hijacking it. What was the prize again?"

"A trip for two to the Bahamas."

Tiff hummed over the phone. "I've got people looking into it. But I don't see what the mob would want with any of that. Especially Marconi. He's got plenty enough dough to take himself on the trip."

Peter ran a hand through his hair, growing more frustrated. "What do they want, then?"

Behind him, Jessica called out, "Peter, I need your help here."

Marconi, wandering closer, smiled wider. Peter narrowed his eyes at the mobster. Something else was bound to happen. He knew it. But what? Nothing that happened here made sense.

"Call me if you learn anything," Peter muttered, then hung up.

"Peter!" Jessica called again.

Grimacing, Peter hurried back. With a glance over everything, he saw the corncakes needed to have their final touches done. He took them from the muffin tins as Jessica added a touch more honey to the chili.

"When you asked me to help you with this, I thought it was because you wanted to do something together, to win that prize together," Jessica snapped at him. "I wish you had told me it was just a front in your most recent investigation."

Peter's head snapped up. "That's not—"

"Just don't talk to me unless it's about the chili," Jessica interrupted.

Peter snapped his jaw shut. How could Jessica not realize how important this was? He kept working while also monitoring their competitors. The weirdly familiar chef beside them was plating his food expertly.

"I didn't think there was anything to investigate," Peter said in a low voice as he grabbed some grated cheese. "Not until Eugene was poisoned. This isn't how I planned this to go, Jessica."

Jessica plated the chili and arranged the corncakes on the edge of the plate. "We'll talk later."

Peter tried to ignore the edge to her tone. It was the same edge in his ex-wife's voice whenever they had an argument. He already knew how that ended. He didn't want to go down the same path as Jessica.

A buzzer rang out, and all the chefs had to step back from their plates.

The Chili Mayor stepped up to the podium. "Thank you, contestants. Before we judge, I just want to let everyone know we received word from the hospital. Eugene Morris is going to be just fine."

Applause answered his declaration. Peter's shoulders sagged in relief.

Jessica stared at her chili, then lifted her face to the sky. Fresh tears glimmered in her eyes. "I'm sorry," she whispered to Peter. "I'm competitive. And I wanted to win this thing. I wanted us to work perfectly together."

Peter sighed and reached cautiously for her hand. "This isn't what I wanted, either. But we will talk later when the emotions are a little less intense. I'm the kind of guy that needs some cool-down time after a fight."

Jessica nodded once. "Just… you're not going to go radio silent on me, right? That's what my ex did. Whenever I disagreed with him, he shut down and refused to talk."

"I will not do that," Peter promised. He squeezed her hand and smiled gently at her. "We will talk."

Jessica gave him a watery smile in return.

By this time, the judges had been moving from station to station, trying the different chilis. They approached Marconi's man cautiously. As the chef proudly explained what he put in the chili, a wave of recognition swept over Peter.

The first judge brought their spoon to their lips.

"Stop!" Peter yelled.

Everyone jolted.

"Stop," Peter repeated, striding forward. "Something's not right here."

CHAPTER
ELEVEN

PINE GROVE CENTENNIAL PARK,
5:10 P.M.

PETER STOPPED in front of the station, blood pumping through his veins stronger. He had figured it out. The contest was rigged, after all! Marconi was behind Eugene being poisoned and Leah's fiery accident. He glared at Marconi, who looked back with an innocent expression.

One judge gave Peter a dirty look. "What is it now?"

"This man shouldn't be part of the cookoff," Peter said, gesturing toward the chef.

The man gave him an affronted look. "Excuse me?"

It all made sense now. The reason this man didn't look like the rest of the mafia types. Why he was so much at ease. Because he wasn't one of Marconi's mobsters.

"Myers, I should have known you weren't done," Donnelly complained as he stomped over. "What is it now? You going to say that he put rats in his chili?"

"I would never!" the chef cried, putting a hand to his chest.

Peter opened his mouth to explain, but Donnelly interrupted him. "I have had it up to here with your posturing and behavior, Myers. If you have no confidence in your skills, you should bow out and let the competition continue."

"If you are quiet for a moment, I'll explain," Peter said.

Donnelly rolled his eyes and gestured for him to talk.

"I—"

Marconi stepped closer. "Is something the problem?"

Peter turned on him. "Yes, there is. And you know there is. You've tried to rig the competition so that your man here would win."

Everyone glanced at each other. Some of them looked annoyed, and others were interested in the unfolding drama. Peter looked over his shoulder, but Jessica was staring at their plates, shoulders hunched. His stomach plummeted. He'd ruined this, hadn't he?

"I rigged the competition?" Marconi repeated. "Why would I do that? I have my own tickets to the Bahamas later this month. I don't need to win any prize."

Peter clenched his jaw. That was the problem. He still hadn't figured out why Marconi wanted to win this competition. He shook his head. "I don't know why but I know how. This is Chef Romario Garridan. He's no novice contestant; he's a formally trained chef with over three restaurants across the continental US and an upcoming TV show."

Donnelly sputtered.

"Romario Garridan?" Jessica slipped from their station to stand next to Peter. "Oh! I see it now. Without that moustache, he looks exactly like the commercials."

Marconi scratched the back of his head as he pushed through the crowd. He came to stand next to Romario, who looked extremely put out.

"All right. He's a classically trained chef. I don't recall saying it any differently. For that matter, I looked over the rules carefully. Nothing in them says the chefs must be novice or home cooks." Marconi cocked his head as he looked at the judges. "But if I'm mistaken, I will gladly withdraw my contestant."

Donnelly huffed. "I don't recall anything in the rules about that."

One by one, the judges shook their heads.

Peter growled low in his throat. "And Eugene being poisoned—"

"I had nothing to do with that. Why would I?" Marconi folded his arms and frowned. "Even if he's won this competition for years, I have a trained professional. I don't need to sabotage anyone... are you just sore that if your theory is right, nobody thought you were enough of a threat to sabotage you?"

"You know what?" Jessica drew herself up next to Peter. "I am certain Verna will not be happy when I tell her about this. She thinks so highly of you, Martin."

Marconi looked stunned.

Peter took a deep breath. He might end up losing his entire relationship with Jessica, but he couldn't trust that Marconi hadn't sabotaged him somehow. It would be just like the mafia to use his chili to poison all the judges and get him put away.

"We're withdrawing from the contest. Do whatever you want," he said, turning on his heel.

He expected Jessica to protest, but she was silent as she followed him back. They put things away, and Peter couldn't bring himself to look at her. She wanted this so badly, and now he'd ruined her chances. As he packed up, his gut twisted even worse. After all the hard work she'd put into this...

Just as they were carrying the last supplies to the car, the Chili Mayor took the podium again.

"It is my great pleasure to announce this year's winner," he called out.

Peter scowled and hurried his steps. He didn't want to witness Marconi's gloating.

"To a chili that was bold, flavorful, and full of character, first prize and the trip for two to the Bahamas goes to... Captain Richard Donnelly, our very own police chief."

Peter's head snapped up. *What?*

"I didn't expect that," Jessica said.

"I... don't know what to say."

Jessica tugged his hand. "Say nothing. Let's just get out of here. I'm starving and can't stand the smell of chili anymore."

CHAPTER
TWELVE
THE MYERS' RESIDENCE

DESPITE WHAT JESSICA had said at the park, by the time they got back to Peter's place, the smell of the chili was so tempting that it was all she wanted to eat. After some discussion, Peter admitted that, since Jessica had been at the station the whole time, nobody could have slipped anything into their chili.

So, now they sat on the couch, staring into the fireplace and eating chili while Sam snoozed at their feet.

"This is fantastic," Peter said. He gave her a rueful smile. "I'm sorry that I unilaterally withdrew us from the competition."

Jessica shook her head. While it had stung at the time, she still understood why he had done it. "There's always next year. And hey, we just had our first major fight. I think we handled it pretty well."

Peter chuckled. "I'm not sure about that. But at least things didn't blow up. I am sorry for being so distracted, leaving you to do it alone."

"Thank you. I'm sorry for letting my competitive streak ruin the fun." Jessica found a nice fat kidney bean and scooped it from the chili. "But the truth is, I was more hurt because you weren't talking to me."

"I'm sorry about that, too. I just thought it was for the best."

Jessica sighed. "I guess there are some things that I can't expect to be told when it comes to your investigations, huh?"

Peter gave her an apologetic look.

"I guess that's something I'll have to get used to," Jessica said. She gave him a bright smile. "Just like you'll have to get used to my crazy competitive streak. There's a pie contest at the Christmas festival. I expect that you and I will do better with that one."

Peter laughed. "Of course!"

They settled into a companionable silence. Jessica smiled as her heart warmed. Maybe, just maybe, they made this work yet.

EPILOGUE
THE TIMMS' RESIDENCE

"POLICE CORRUPTION, that's what it is," Romario grumbled into his bowl of chili as he sulked in the corner. Several of the cats lounged about him. "My chili is better than any police chief's. I bet he threatened them. Bribed them."

Marconi fought the urge to threaten the celebrity chef to get him to shut up. Everything had gone exactly how Marconi wanted it to. Everything, from Peter's distraction to the outcome of the cookoff.

He savored the taste of chili on his tongue, knowing that it would be a while before he could enjoy something like this again. The vet's last parting shot at him still made him wince. But Aunt Verna didn't understand these things. She would be disappointed in him, yes... but Marconi couldn't let that distract him.

Russo came into the room, a cat perched on his shoulders. He grinned with a swagger as he brought a laptop over to Marconi.

"Did you get what I sent you for?" Marconi asked, wiping all trace of emotion from his face and voice.

"Sure did," Russo crowed. He set the laptop down and opened it up. "It was just like you said. We had to give that dog the steak you prepped, and it was out like a light."

"Let me see." Marconi leaned back in his chair, the warmth of the chili twisting in his gut now. Great. Just what he needed. He'd gone for years without having a conscience; there was no reason for one to bug him now.

Russo opened the laptop and hit a few buttons. Within a few moments, the live footage from Peter's house flickered to life. It was an image of the living room. From the warm, flickering glow, the only light came from a fire.

Sitting on an old, worn couch were Peter and that vet woman. Their hands twined together as they leaned in, sharing a kiss.

I told you to watch your back, Myers, Marconi thought grimly. "Good work, men. We got what we came for."

The End

Best Man Down

A PINE GROVE MYSTERY

DAISY LANDISH

PROLOGUE
THE MYERS' RESIDENCE

PETER WHISTLED as he checked through his suitcase, packed for his coming vacation. Everything was ready to go, and this was a vacation he was very ready to take. So much had happened here in Pine Grove the last few months that it made his head spin. Winter had finally settled in, making everything cold and blustering.

But that was just one perk of this trip. The weather in Florida was hot and balmy. Still Lake would provide plenty of recreational activities that weren't possible in New England at this time of year. He hadn't been this excited about a trip in years.

Sam whined from where he lay next to the empty fireplace, looking up at Peter with doleful eyes.

"Everything's fine, Sam," Peter told him. "Eugene will come and look after you while I'm gone. He'll take you on walks, and since he doesn't work, you'll be able to sit with him and watch TV all day. Won't that be nice?"

"Woof," said Sam, beating his tail once on the ground.

Peter smiled at his dog and crouched next to him. It was the first time since getting Sam that he'd be away for more than a few hours, and he had to admit he found himself quite nervous at the prospect. It reminded him of how jittery he was when his oldest was born and he had to return to work for the first time.

"I was much more of a wreck then," he told Sam, scratching behind his ears. "The wedding is only for a few days; I'll be back before you know it. Nothing to be nervous about."

Sam's nose wiggled, and he said, "Woof!"

"I know it's with Jessica. But that's not why you can't come. You wouldn't want to be cooped up in an airplane for hours just to be cooped up in a strange hotel room most of the time, right?" Peter stroked Sam's soft head. "I'm only going with her as a favor. Like friends do."

He could have sworn that Sam rolled his eyes at that moment.

"We're friends," Peter insisted. "And nothing more than friends."

"Woof," Sam said doubtfully.

Peter shook his head as he returned to his packing. Sam wasn't being doubtful. The dog didn't even understand what he was saying, let alone think there was something more between Peter and Jessica than friendship. They were friends... albeit friends who kissed sometimes.

But kissing didn't mean they weren't friends, right?

Being invited as her plus-one at a wedding certainly put more pressure on their relationship. Friendship. Peter cleared his throat as he closed his suitcase, satisfied that he had everything he would need.

"Friendship is a type of relationship," he told Sam. "And that's what we have—a friendship. A wonderful friendship, mind you. But it is a friendship. I will not wreck that. You wouldn't know, but I haven't been divorced for long. Melanie, my ex-wife, was an exceptional woman. It's not her fault we divorced. It's not mine, either. We just moved too fast, and then...."

Peter shook his head, his heart growing heavy as he thought of his ex-wife and his two adult children. Rina and Matt still needed to meet Jessica. He would have to have their opinions on her before he pursued anything. The last thing he wanted was to fall in love, only to drive a wedge between him and his children.

"I need to stop thinking," he told Sam, crouching to pet his head. "I'll be back before you know it. Be good for Eugene, okay?"

"Woof," Sam said.

Peter smiled. He picked up his suitcase and headed out the door.

This was just the vacation he needed. All these questions about relationships and friendships would have to wait.

<hr>

THE TIMMS' Residence

Short and squat, Marconi loosened his belt, sighing as the pressure on his gut eased. He would pack even more weight if Aunt Verna kept feeding him so much good, rich food. He knew he ought to tell her enough was enough; he needed to watch what he ate, but it just felt too good to be looked after.

Besides, Aunt Verna wasn't the sort of woman you could say no to quickly.

The door of the Myers house swung shut as Peter left. Marconi watched the small image from the hidden camera in Peter's house. So, Myers was off to Still Lake for a wedding with Jessica Stern.

"Just friends, ha!" Marconi shook his head. "Maybe I should plan a fishing trip for this weekend."

CHAPTER
ONE
THE CESSNA

THE TWIN-ENGINE PLANE cruised through the air, the land beneath slowly turning from white and brown to greener fields. Every time Peter checked the external temperatures, it was warmer. He grinned, glad that the weather cooperated for this flight. It wasn't easy to tell in winter if he'd be able to get off the ground safely or not.

A few dark clouds were forming on the horizon, but nothing to be worried about.

It felt so right to have Jessica sitting in the copilot seat. She'd taken off her shoes, and now her feet were nestled in fuzzy slippers while she had one of those Snuggie blankets tucked in tight around her with her arms through the sleeves. Her eyes were alight with amazement even though they had been in the air for some time.

"I can't tell you how much I'm looking forward to this trip," Jessica told him as she glanced over at him. She grinned widely, her excitement palpable.

"Me, too," Peter said. They were at a cruising altitude, allowing him to spare some attention to Jessica. "I'm eager for fishing and hiking. No snow! I'm going to thaw out finally."

Jessica laughed, a sound that lightened Peter's heart. "Not going to lie; I'm going to miss the snow a little. But everything else makes up for it. Two days off work, far enough away that I can't be called in for an emergency. I'm not sure the last time I was this far from Pine Grove."

"Really? I thought you went to conferences regularly."

Jessica shrugged. "These days, they're all virtual. So, no need to leave my house."

"Well, then! I'll make it my mission to keep us both entertained and relaxed." Peter grinned.

She elbowed him. "Not too much, though. You're my ride home, remember... I don't want you to get so relaxed and thawed out that you decide not to fly me back."

The teasing glint in her eye made him want to kiss her. Peter allowed himself to fall into that fantasy for a moment, thinking about how soft her lips were and how right it felt when he was close to Jessica. It was so comfortable with her, and more than that. It made sense to him...

He cleared his throat and pushed those thoughts aside. Friends. He didn't want to ruin that. "Are you sure it's all right for me to be with you at your brother's wedding? People might get the wrong idea."

"Wrong idea?"

"You know. That things between us are more than they are?" Peter winced.

Jessica laughed. "That's the big-time lawyer eloquence, huh? But don't worry about it. I don't care what other people think... it's good to have a few rumors swirling around you from time to time, anyway. I just want a friend to keep me company."

"If you're sure," Peter said doubtfully.

"Why wouldn't I be?"

Peter double-checked Jessica's expression, not sure if she was still teasing or getting annoyed. Her eyebrows were drawn together as though she was confused. His shoulders relaxed slightly. At the end of his relationship with Melanie, everything appeared to be an argument. The two of them had somehow forgotten to communicate.

Sometimes, Peter was worried that his friendship with Jessica would end the same way, that it was his fault.

"I guess I'm just nervous," he finally said.

Jessica shook her head with a slight smile. "Don't worry. I'm not standing up at the wedding, and I doubt many people will be pumping me for information about my life. Honestly, I don't know my extended family that well. My baby brother wouldn't get married without inviting me, but he's always been the social butterfly, not me."

"So, you don't need a partner for it?"

"Nope."

"Then why invite me?"

Jessica rolled her eyes. "Peter. I will not know most of the people there. I want a friend around, so I don't get bored out of my mind. I'm inviting you along because you've been moaning about wanting to go fishing forever. I thought maybe I'd do something nice for you, too. Unless the storms chase the fish away."

Her brow furrowed with worry.

Peter turned back to the skies in front of them. The few wispy dark clouds he'd noticed rapidly gained more form, becoming thicker and darker. His hands clenched around the steering wheel. He should have been paying better attention… these weren't regular storm clouds.

His jaw tightened as he scanned the ground, hoping to find someplace to set the Cessna down safely. The plane shuddered, then jerked as a sudden crosswind hit them. He suddenly realized that the wind had been at their backs this time, blowing them toward the storm faster than he expected.

"Make sure your seatbelt is tight," he instructed Jessica, keeping his tone firm and calm. The last thing either of them needed in this situation was to panic. "This is going to be a bumpy ride."

CHAPTER
TWO
THE CESSNA

THE PLANE BUCKED AND THRASHED, but Peter forced himself to remain calm, navigating through the storm. He had got above most of it, but the winds were still strong. Below them, all he could see were dark clouds. He kept the plane on course, though, focused on his job.

Jessica was silent in her seat, eyes closed and breathing deeply. Peter could sense her tension but couldn't spare any thoughts to soothing her.

Soon, they had passed the storm. It wasn't a large group of clouds, only a few miles long. Peter released a heavy breath. The wind was still something to contend with, but as he dipped the nose of the plane to get back to a lower elevation, even that eased.

"We're almost there," he promised Jessica.

She opened her eyes and let out a shuddering breath. Quickly, she pulled her pack from under her seat and grabbed her water bottle. "Does that happen often?"

Peter grimaced. "No. Sorry, that was my fault. I should have paid more attention. Looks like clear skies for the rest of the trip, though."

"Good," Jessica mumbled.

"Sorry," he said again.

Jessica didn't seem to hear him.

It was less than half an hour before they went through the storm when they landed. Clouds had started to form above them once more, and the runway was getting spotted with raindrops. The drizzle got heavier, and Peter was grateful they could touch down when they did.

Jessica sagged into her seat as Peter taxied to a stop, then laughed. "That was an adventure, wasn't it?"

Peter was surprised at how lightly she took their 'adventure.' "I suppose, yeah."

"Hopefully, the weather will be clear when we head home," Jessica continued as she moved off her Snuggie. "I missed seeing the scenery. It looks so cool from the air."

Peter smiled at her in appreciation, then turned the plane off. They got out and were almost instantly swarmed by a handful of people running across the tarmac. They greeted Jessica enthusiastically and bombarded her with questions as she attempted to introduce Peter.

Peter was getting overwhelmed by their friendliness when finally, they moved away. He used the excuse of needing to check over the plane before he joined them. It was the truth, of course, but after the harrowing flight, he also needed some time to decompress before being social.

The plane had sustained no noticeable damage. Peter did the after-flight check and cleanup, ensuring everything was in order. Once that was done, he unloaded his and Jessica's luggage. They each had a single suitcase, more than enough for a weekend. Secretly, Peter hoped this could end up being a little more than a weekend.

Although Jessica had her veterinary practice, she probably would not want to take any extra time.

Peter shook his head. He'd been keeping busy, but perhaps he should find another job. Retirement didn't seem to suit him all too well.

As he started toward the cars where Jessica's family waited, he spotted a person in the nearest hanger staring at him. When Peter turned his head to see him more clearly, the man turned quickly away. Embarrassed to be caught staring, or something more sinister?

Peter shook the thought off. He was getting paranoid. Nobody here knew him. It was a worker or something like that. There was no need to see shadows where there were none... he had enough troubles in Pine Grove with all the investigations he'd been taking up.

This was a vacation, and nothing was going to go wrong here.

CHAPTER
THREE
STILL LAKE RESORT

THAT NIGHT, Peter and Jessica were supposed to slip out and get dinner together, but just as he was about to head down to the car rental, Jessica knocked on his door. Her expression was twisted in regret as she gave him an apologetic smile.

"It appears I'm more of a central guest than I realized," she told him. "I've been invited to be part of the bachelorette party. I don't want to be rude to them... are you going to be okay on your own for dinner?"

Peter laughed. "Don't worry about it. I'm plenty capable of taking care of myself."

"You sure?" Jessica asked, grimacing.

Peter lowered his voice conspiratorially. "Are you looking for an excuse to skip the bachelorette party?"

Jessica considered the question for a moment before she shook her head sadly. "No. I'm kind of excited about it. I didn't want to abandon you after dragging you out here."

"You twisted my arm," Peter teased. "Pulling me away from all that cold snow to this beautiful climate... yep, you dragged me."

Jessica rolled her eyes.

"Go on and have fun," Peter urged. No, he didn't want to be alone tonight; he had been looking forward to taking Jessica to dinner. They usually just made food together at his place. It seemed like he would have to wait on that, though.

It's what friends do; he reminded himself. *And even romantic partners need to feel free to have fun on their own from time to time."*

Jessica hugged him. "I'll call around ten to see how you're doing. And if I need an excuse to leave the party, I'll talk about watermelons, okay?"

Peter snorted but nodded. "Sounds good. Have fun."

She waved as she skipped down the hallway toward her room. The bride's family owned this hotel resort and booked every single room for the wedding. It was a much larger affair than Peter had thought it would be.

Still, he was happy that Jessica knew so many guests. It gave him a chance to see her more outside of her element. In the vet's office, she was always calm and in control, and while it was just the two of them, she was relaxed and playful. When they had entered the chili cooking contest together, he'd seen a new, competitive side to her.

He hoped to learn more about her this weekend as well.

Since he now went out alone, Peter no longer wanted to go to the upscale restaurant he'd chosen previously. He changed out of the semi-formal attire he'd put on, switching to jeans and a t-shirt, and headed for a local bar within walking distance.

As soon as he got into the bar, he realized his mistake. The bride was having her bachelorette party in the hotel dining room—the bachelor party was here. And it was already in full swing, with the smell of beer and steaks penetrating the air.

"You made it!" a jovial voice cried.

Peter turned to see the groom, Michael, stumble toward him. A huge smile was plastered on his face as he slammed his hand into Peter's back in a welcoming gesture.

"I—excuse me," Peter said, trying to hide his confusion. "I didn't realize you were having your party here. I'll just—"

"Didn't you get an invitation?" Michael's face fell. "Cory! Cory, why didn't my big sister's guest get an invitation?"

The best man, sitting in a corner booth looking at his phone, glanced up. "Uh. Must have slipped my mind."

He turned back to his phone, a furrow on his brow.

Peter was distracted as Michael laughed and slapped his back again. "See there? You should have gotten an invitation. I want to get to know you better if you spend time with my big sister."

That was a good point. Come to think of it, that could very well be why Jessica invited him along. He needed to get to know her family as much as she needed to get to know his. Besides, these young men were all acting wild and drunk already. They needed a designated driver here.

It wasn't long after before the only woman in the bar appeared. She wore a short, body-hugging black skirt paired with a white shirt with a low-plunging neckline. Peter would have mistaken her for a server at the bar, except for the nine-inch heels she wore. The young men started whistling.

Michael, who was trying to tell Peter that he could shoot pool better while drunk than sober, didn't notice the woman. Peter frowned as she zeroed in on the groom. This wasn't the bride; he knew that.

The woman marched over. As Michael turned to see whom Peter was looking at, she grabbed him and started trying to kiss him. Peter jumped in as Michael cried out in protest. She yanked his shirt, trying to pull him closer. Peter pushed between the two of them.

"Leave us alone. Mikey and I have lots to talk about," the woman purred, flicking open the next button of her shirt. She wore a lacy red bra underneath.

Michael spluttered.

Peter opened his mouth, but before saying anything, Cory was there. He grabbed the woman's arm and dragged her toward the door.

"Hey," she cried.

"Michael isn't interested in you," Cory seethed at her, releasing her but still blocking her way. "You're not welcome here. Leave."

The young woman threw her head, her curly hair wafting around her. She put her hands on her hips as she lifted her lip in a sneer. "You'll regret this, Cory Atkins. All of you will regret this. You'll see. You'll get what's coming to you. It's only fair, given what you did!"

"LEAVE!" Cory howled, pointing at the door.

She rolled her eyes, stomped her foot, and headed out.

Peter turned back to Michael, who was rubbing his hand over his mouth as though trying to erase the kiss that hadn't happened. He looked angry, but when he met Peter's gaze, he tried to pull off a carefree grin.

"Back to the party," Michael cried into the silent bar.

A lot of cheering and drinking met this remark.

Peter shook his head as he slid into a booth, ready to have a moment aside. Kids. He was glad he wasn't caught up in this sort of drama anymore. But it seemed like Michael would not let this woman, whoever she was, upset him. He was already back to partying, attempting to shoot pool with a chopstick.

Peter chuckled. Ah, yes. He remembered those days.

CHAPTER
FOUR
STILL LAKE RESORT

THE FOLLOWING DAY, Peter woke up just before dawn. By the time ten rolled around the previous night, he and Jessica had been partied out. They used each other as an excuse to leave their respective festivities and then had some quiet time on Jessica's balcony playing Uno until they were ready for sleep.

Jessica wasn't an early riser, and so would meet Peter later. As for him, he knew that this would be the best time to get some peace out on the lake. He wanted to catch at least one fish on this trip.

Still, he paused when he crept past Jessica's door. The bachelor party events last night had drawn to the forefront all the memories he'd have of his own wedding decades ago. If his relationship with Jessica was going to develop into romance, it was something they needed to talk about.

He continued without knocking. While having a peaceful morning together would be an ideal time to have the relationship talk, it would not happen when she was still half-asleep.

Outside, a thick fog rose over the lake. It gave the air a damp, spooky feeling. Peter almost returned to his warm hotel room but headed for the docks instead. He'd come to fish, and it was far colder in New England than here!

Various row boats, canoes, and kayaks were pulled out of the water, resting upside down at the shoreline. Peter headed over there. As he picked out a beautiful rowboat, his foot knocked against something.

He looked down and gasped. A man lay half in the water. His face was pressed into the sand, barely out of the waves. His hair was dark and matted with blood. Peter quickly dropped to his knees. He cradled the man's neck with one hand as he turned him over to get him out of the water.

Peter stifled another gasp. It was Cory Atkins, the best man. His skin was cold to the touch, but he was still breathing, if barely. The frigid lake water continued to lap at the unconscious man's body.

"Cory, it's Peter Myers," he said, keeping his voice loud but calm. "I'm going to pull you out of the water."

Carefully, Peter looped his arms through Cory's and pulled him up the beach, just far enough so the water would no longer sap his warmth; then Peter stripped off his own jacket and laid it over the shivering man.

"I need help," he yelled toward the resort. "Help!"

CHAPTER
FIVE

JESSICA RUBBED one hand over her eyes as she handed Michael a coffee. Everything was in disarray this morning since Peter had discovered Cory in the lake. The bride, Arista, had nearly broken down, and Michael was still trying to console her.

"Is there anything I can get for you?" Jessica asked the red-eyed blonde.

Arista shook her head, sniffing as she dabbed at her eyes. Either she had the world's best mascara, or her eyelashes naturally grew in that thick and dark. "Thank you, but I should stick with water. I just can't believe it. Cory was never the kind to overindulge like that. He hasn't gotten drunk once in the years I've known him."

"Cory can be pretty uptight," Michael chuckled nervously.

"I told you not to make him your best man," Arista said, her tone suddenly vicious. "I told you it wouldn't be any good."

Michael grit his teeth. "So, this is my fault?"

"No. I just meant—I don't know. I'm just worried for him."

Jessica cleared her throat. "If you don't need anything, I think I should find Peter."

Arista looked up at her with a surprised expression, like she had forgotten Jessica was there. "Oh. Of course. See to your guest."

Jessica nodded once, feeling awkward. Michael was clearly giving her a look that he wanted to talk with his bride alone, but as she stepped back, Arista's hand shot out and grabbed her sleeve.

"I just want to say thank you for being here. It means so much to Michael and me. I just wanted this to be perfect... and now for the best man to get so plastered that he fell into the lake?" She shook her head and dropped Jessica's sleeve. "I just don't get it."

"We were having fun last night," Michael said, rubbing Arista's arms.

Arista shook her head miserably and started sobbing again.

Jessica frowned. The paramedics hadn't been able to promise anything about Cory's condition, but he was alive when they took him to the hospital; his parents were waiting there with him while the rest of the wedding party remained at the resort.

However, Michael was giving her that look again. Jessica mumbled some appropriate sympathies and slipped away as Arista buried her face in Michael's shoulder.

She hadn't seen Peter in a while, but Jessica thought she knew where to find him. Her hunch was proven right when she headed for the lake to find him at the docks, taking pictures with his phone. She sighed internally.

One of the major reasons she wanted to bring him on this trip was to finally have the time and space to discuss what was between them. Every time she thought they were getting closer, it seemed like something else pushed between them. Now with this accident... she knew Peter. He wasn't going just to let it lie.

"Hey," she called when she got close enough.

Peter looked up. "Any word from the hospital?"

"Not yet." Jessica stopped next to him. "What are you looking for?"

Peter slid his phone into his pocket. "Just making sure I missed nothing. How well do you know Cory?"

Jessica got a twisting feeling in her stomach at the question. It was going to turn into an interrogation. "Not well. I'm twelve years older than Cory, and he was born just after our parents' divorce. I stayed with my dad mostly, and he stayed with my mom. We've never been close. I don't really know his friends."

"So, you don't know how long Michael and Cory knew each other?"

"Not really. I think they met in college?"

"Hmmm." Peter ran a hand through his hair, which he often did when brooding. "I overheard a few bridesmaids saying that they couldn't believe Cory would pull something like this. It seemed like they had little an opinion of him."

Jessica glanced at him uneasily. She didn't want to be the one spreading rumors, but she had something to add. "Uh... well, Arista was just saying something about knowing him for years and that he's not the kind to get blackout drunk."

Peter clucked his tongue as he gazed over the water.

"She also seemed to think it was a bad idea for Michael to have him as best man," Jessica continued reluctantly. "But I don't know what it's all about."

"When I left the bachelor party, things were still in full swing. What about the bachelorette party?"

Jessica grimaced. She didn't want to admit that she had felt like the chaperone to these women who were much younger than her. The conversation hadn't been to her liking, and neither had the plans. It appeared the only thing any of them wanted to do was get drunk.

"After the bride's parents cut off the alcohol at the resort, they decided to all get dressed in these outlandish costumes and go out to some swanky place for food and more drinks. They came back to the resort at about three, I think. They woke me up."

Peter nodded. "I heard some crying during the night."

"I checked on them to ensure they were all returning to their rooms. They were messy," Jessica admitted, wrinkling her nose. "I couldn't believe it."

"Messy?"

"Arista was so wasted she could hardly walk, and the rest weren't much better." She wrinkled her nose. "If I'm honest, I never really liked Arista's friends. She's a nice enough woman, but her friends are... off-putting. They seem to bring out the worst in her."

"I see. This isn't good."

How did she know he was going to say that? Jessica cupped her face in her hands, her heart sinking. "Why?"

Peter jerked her chin. "It looks like this is a criminal matter."

Jessica turned. Any leftover hope of a quiet weekend went straight out the window when she saw a police officer approaching.

CHAPTER
SIX
STILL LAKE RESORT

THE POLICE OFFICER, Detective Cray, shooed Peter and Jessica back to the hotel until he was ready to talk to them. Peter wasn't happy with how quickly he dismissed them, especially as Peter had been the one to find Cory. He tried to give the detective some information, but Cray only told him more firmly to get back to the hotel.

Jessica was quiet as they walked back. Her expression was troubled, and understandably so.

Peter reached for her hand. "I'm sure it will be resolved in time for the wedding to proceed."

"Is that even a good idea?" Jessica murmured.

Peter had no answer. They entered the hotel lobby to find it empty. Everyone must have returned to their rooms. He ran a hand through his hair, and Jessica tugged him toward a couple of stuffed leather chairs to one side of the lobby.

"I guess we'll just wait until he wants to talk to us," Jessica murmured, subdued. Her shoulders slumped forward. "The last thing I wanted this weekend was another mystery to pop up."

"Yeah. I know."

Jessica chewed her lip. "I love that you are always figuring things out. You take a personal interest in people and try to help them solve their problems. I just don't like how often stuff has been happening."

"I can't control that."

"I know. And I don't want to ask you to ignore it when you see something that needs fixing." Jessica slumped in her chair. "Maybe I'm too tired for this conversation. My thoughts just keep going in circles. I just… it's like with my work. I get called off for emergencies that need me far more often than I'd like. But I'm not going to stop."

Peter took her hand in his, squeezing lightly. "I understand what you mean. Sometimes I wonder if I'm sane with these investigations I find myself part of."

Jessica gave him a strained smile. "Oh, you're sane. It's just your drive. You're a fixer."

The detective entered the lobby. Peter immediately stood to approach, but Cray waved him off. "When I'm ready."

He spoke to the desk clerk in a low voice, and the clerk made a few calls. Soon, Michael and his groomsmen were in the lobby, answering questions. Peter stayed where he was, watching Detective Cray work. He was slick, getting the groomsmen to divulge more information than they thought.

But they were hiding something. There was a caginess to their answers that Peter knew all too well.

When the detective dismissed the groomsmen, he finally turned to Peter. He strode over and offered a hand. "Mr. Myers. I'm sorry to keep you waiting for so long."

"It's all right," Peter said graciously. This was yet another tactic on the Detective's part. "What would you like to know?"

Cray glanced over his notepad, where he had been writing. "Hmmm. Well, you can start with anything the groomsmen may have missed. I understand you were at the bachelor party?"

How did he know that already? Nobody here had told him. Peter fought to keep the surprise off his face. "Yes, actually. A woman showed up at the party and accosted Michael, the groom. Cory kicked her out, and she said something along the lines of 'I'll make you pay for what you did.' I'm not sure if she was talking to Cory or Michael, though."

"Can you describe her?"

Peter did so.

"Ah! That's Kaia Lister," Cray chuckled. "Kaia's got quite the repu-tation around town. She's always making threats but doesn't have the gumption to go through with them. She likes to start trouble, not finish it."

Peter frowned at Cray. "What do you mean?"

"I mean, she's not the person I'm looking for." Cray grinned, his even white teeth flashing. "An itty-bitty thing like her working at the Roundhouse couldn't brain a man the size of Cory Atkins and throw him in the lake."

CHAPTER
SEVEN
STILL LAKE RESORT

JESSICA FOUND Michael at the hotel bar, nursing along a shot of whiskey. From his disheveled appearance, she knew he was still overcoming a hangover from the previous night. She had to shake her head as she approached. Everything seemed out of hand now.

The only thing she could think of was to fix this for her baby brother. And how better to do that than to aid Peter in his investigation? Right now, the wedding party didn't seem to think what happened to Cory was anything but an accident. She had to pick out more information before they figured it out.

"Hey," she greeted as she slid onto the stool next to him. "Where's Arista?"

"Hmm? Oh. Oh, her parents took her back to her room so she could calm down. They're insisting we keep going with the wedding as scheduled."

Jessica checked her watch discreetly. The wedding was supposed to be at five tonight. It was currently ten in the morning. She blew out a heavy breath.

"I can't believe they think we should get married while Cory's in the hospital. I don't even know if he will be okay yet, and they're expecting me to dress up and act like nothing is happening."

"I can talk to them," Jessica suggested. "I can't imagine they won't understand that you want to make sure that your best man is going to recover before you have your wedding."

Michael silently sipped his whiskey. There was a dark, brooding expression on his face that Jessica didn't like. How well did he really know his bride and her family? What sort of people would push ahead a party like this after what happened?

That would have to wait, though. She needed information about who would have it out for his best man.

"I can't remember when you and Cory met. It was in college, right?"

"Nah. Senior year of high school. I dated his sister for a while."

"His sister?" Jessica arched a brow. "And you two stayed friends even after you broke up?"

Michael gave her a pained look. "His sister moved to London for her schooling and ended things with me because I wouldn't go with her."

That sounded reasonable. They would have been so young, and Jessica believed nobody would give up their best education for romance. Not that she was going to say it.

"Cory was furious with her. They'd never really been close, and I guess that was the final straw... Cory went through a bad breakup at the same time, his girlfriend cheated on him, and I guess we just bonded as we got over it."

"Right. And how long has Arista known him?"

"I dunno, really. I know her parents and his parents go to the same church, and that's all." Michael frowned at his whiskey glass. "Though, come to think of it, I don't get what she was talking about earlier."

Jessica leaned in. "You mean he gets drunk a lot?"

"Drunk, no. He doesn't do that." Michael replied cagily.

"So, what does he do?"

"He has fun. He doesn't always know when to stop. He probably went down to the lake to swim and tripped." Michael tipped back his whiskey, grimaced, and set the shot glass down. "I better go get ready for the wedding."

"Michael—"

"Arista's right. I shouldn't have brought him. I should have known he'd bring… bad luck with him." Michael ducked his head and hurried away.

Jessica closed her eyes. Exhaustion played on her brain, but if there was one thing she took from this conversation, it was that Cory Atkins brought more than bad luck with him. The only question was, what sort of drugs had he got? And was he just a user, or was he a dealer, too?

I have to tell Peter.

CHAPTER
EIGHT

THE TROUT DINER AND DRIVE-THROUGH

THE DINER WAS PACKED with the lunch rush when Peter entered. Only one table was still open, and he took a seat. His gaze skimmed over the servers who were busy bustling from table to table. He soon found his target.

Kaia Lister was indeed petite. Without her insanely high heels, she would only reach Peter's shoulder. Today, rather than the vixen's outfit she had on from last night, she wore black slacks and a white blouse paired with a blue scarf around her neck to hide any cleavage that might be shown.

He waved her over.

The young woman smiled widely until she got a good look at him. Then she stopped dead, a panicked look coming to her eyes. "Uh... uh... what can I get for you?"

Peter glanced at the menu. "A coffee to start with. I'll need to look over the menu. Anything you suggest?"

"Well, the clam chowder is delicious. I have it every day." Kaia was struggling to keep a professional demeanor.

Good, she recognized him. This would make things a lot easier. Peter set the menu aside. "And what were you doing at Michael's bachelor party last night?"

Kaia's cheeks turned pink. "Nothing. I mean, it was my last-ditch attempt to win him back. But I was drunk; it didn't mean anything."

"I suppose we were all a little drunk," Peter said evenly. "You know that what you did, putting her hands on him without his consent, constitutes sexual assault, right?"

"How was that—" Kaia spluttered. "You're crazy."

"No, I'm a lawyer."

Kaia's face turned ashen. "*What?*"

People were staring, but Peter paid them no mind. He propped his elbows on the table. "You said you were there to win him back. But when you were leaving, you made some nasty threats toward him."

"I wasn't threatening Michael," Kaia protested.

"Ah, so it was Cory you were threatening?"

"Yes! I mean—no. I was drunk. I didn't mean it." She glanced around, her shoulders hunching inward. It was clear she would rather have been anywhere else but here. "Look, I know what Cory did. He won't get away with it again."

Peter narrowed his eyes at her. She didn't seem like a criminal mastermind, but he'd learned long ago that looks could be deceiving. "What exactly did Cory do that you needed to get revenge on him for?"

"Nothing."

"Kaia, the truth always comes out."

Kaia's nostrils flared. She glanced around again, but there was a gleam in her eye, almost as though she was secretly enjoying the attention. Odd. When she looked back at Peter, the look was gone. His eyes narrowed further. Was she putting on an act?

"Cory was a jerk, okay? He turned Michael against me. Sleeping with him was a mistake. He was messed up and deserved whatever happens to him."

Peter stood. "I don't think I will get anything, after all, Miss Lister." He pulled on his coat, but before he headed for the door, he looked her once more in the eye. "And something has already happened to him."

She showed no emotion. But did that mean she already knew, or she didn't care?

CHAPTER
NINE
STILL LAKE RESORT

ONE O'CLOCK

The wedding was supposed to be in four hours, not that Jessica thought it should be going ahead for any reason. She searched everywhere in the resort and saw no sign of Peter. She had a terrible feeling about all of this and needed to talk about Cory's habits with him so she could give Michael a reason to delay the wedding.

She didn't like that the bride's family was pushing hard for them to continue despite the circumstances. Anyone with empathy would just step back and allow the wedding party to breathe a little before continuing with such an important event.

"Wish I could just step in and tell them we're canceling for now," Jessica groused as she headed down to the lake.

Unfortunately, she already knew that would only push Michael into insisting the wedding take place. Despite their attempts to repair their relationship, he still pushed back against anything she told him.

To her relief, she found Peter was back at the scene where Cody had been found. He was standing ankle-deep in water, poking around the mud. Jessica took a moment to admire what a striking figure he made; his pants rolled up to his knees and an intense expression on his face.

He seemed to suddenly sense he was being watched, and his head jerked up. Relief crossed his features when he saw her approaching.

Only to fall into chagrin. "I should have told you where I was going."

"Probably," Jessica agreed as she kicked off her shoes and waded into the water. "What are we looking for?"

"We?"

"Yes. I want to find out what is going on, too. And I figure that since these mysteries are something you'll keep finding and solving, the best way to spend time with you during these cases is to help the investigation."

Peter seemed surprised at this, but he grinned all the same. "I'd love the help. So, I found the woman who tried to kiss Michael last night. Her name is Kaia, and apparently, she and Michael used to date. She claims Cory poisoned Michael against her and admitted she slept with Cory... not sure which came first, though."

Jessica processed that information. She waded deeper into the water, poking around for anything that looked out of place. "So, she cheated on Michael with Cory and then blamed Cory for it... nice girl."

"Or Cory turned Michael against her, then convinced her to sleep with him under the guise of revenge," Peter offered.

"I suppose." Jessica grimaced. "I think Cory's into drugs."

"Drugs?"

"Just some things Michael was saying and how he said it. I don't have any proof, but it makes sense based on some of the stuff I've seen from him in the past." Jessica paused and rubbed her eyes. She didn't like any of this, but if they were going to figure it out before the wedding, they had to share everything. "Detective Cray was back earlier. He assured everyone that it looked like a terrible accident."

Peter scowled. "And here I thought he would be sharper than Donnelly and the fools in Pine Grove."

"Yeah. I don't buy it, either. Could it be some sort of drug deal gone wrong?"

"Maybe. If we get the police to open their investigation again, we'll have to find something to bring to them, though."

"Like what?" Jessica asked.

She stepped forward, and a sharp pain stabbed into the heel of her foot. With a cry of shock and pain, she jumped back. Something stuck to her foot, and she toppled over in her attempts to balance on her toes to prevent it from driving further into her heel.

Peter caught her, scooping her out of the water. The thing popped off her foot and fell with a splash. Jessica saw a black triangular shape below the water.

"Wait!" she cried as Peter started wading toward the shore. "Get that before we lose it again."

Peter lowered her to the sand and waded back into the lake. Jessica checked her foot as he searched for the thing that stabbed her. No mark was left. She wiped the water from her heel and was relieved when the pain diminished. It hadn't punctured skin, at least.

"What is it?" she called out as Peter bent over.

He brought the triangular thing over to her. "It's the heel of a shoe. No telling how long it's been there, though."

"Wrong." Jessica took the heel from him. It was a high stiletto type that always seemed like a deadly weapon to her. "It wasn't that deep in the mud. It can't have gone in that long ago. Otherwise, it would have been pulled out or buried deeper."

Peter frowned. "Kaia was wearing heels last night."

Jessica grabbed her shoes and shoved her wet feet into them. Excitement pulsed through her veins. "We need to get back to the diner!"

CHAPTER
TEN

THE TROUT DINER AND DRIVE-THROUGH

PETER WAITED OUTSIDE in the car for Jessica's signal. Kaia knew his face and would probably make up some story about him to avoid talking to him. She wouldn't know Jessica, though, and so she went in alone to do some recon.

To his surprise, the door opened, and Jessica strode out toward the car. He frowned as he watched her angry movements. Something had gone wrong.

Jessica slid into the passenger-side seat. "She's not there. I waited for a while but didn't see anyone who matched your description. So I pretended I was a new hire and snuck into the back to check their schedule. Her shift is over."

"Shoot," Peter grumbled. He rested his forehead against the steering wheel. What were they going to do now? His eyes shot open. "Detective Cray mentioned she worked at the Roundhouse."

"I know that place! Well, not personally, but Michael told me all about it. Let's go; I'll get the directions." Jessica pulled her phone from her pocket. "Michael said it's the best nightclub in town. Posh. Great music, great food, great booze, according to him. He told me he and Cory go there all the time."

Peter followed her directions as they made their way through the small resort town. His mind whirled, but he stopped making any assumptions; he needed just a bit more information.

"Same thing?" Jessica asked when they arrived. Her face was flushed with excitement, making her look even more beautiful. "I go in first, and you follow?"

"Yeah," Peter agreed.

She grinned and jumped out of the car. She wasn't dressed for nightclubbing, but Peter doubted the club would still be open for business this early in the day. He checked his watch—only an hour left until the wedding.

He grabbed his phone and called Detective Cray. "Cory Atkins had a head injury. What caused it?"

"What?" Cray asked, sounding cross.

"What caused his head injury?"

"The rocks. We found one with his blood on it. He tripped and fell."

"Thanks." Peter hung up even as Cray tried to demand what was going on. He hadn't heard about the evidence they found, so Peter wasn't eager to share this information now.

He headed in after Jessica. As he stepped inside, he saw a line of young women cleaning and prepping various areas of the club. They all wore tight, short black skirts, white shirts with plunging necklines that showed off a peek of red lace, and nine-inch heels.

What has Kaia said to him? About knowing something?

Jessica stood at the hostess's stand, arguing with the hostess. Peter joined them in time to hear the hostess insist that she couldn't divulge any of her employee's schedules.

"Kaia called out, though, didn't she?" Peter asked. "Because she needs to replace her heels."

The hostess opened her mouth and closed it quickly.

"Never mind about that," Peter continued. "Was there a bachelorette party here last night?"

Jessica gave him a puzzled look.

Trust me. Peter hoped she got the message.

The hostess snorted, putting her hands on her hips. "There certainly was. Because her family runs the resort, that stuck-up brat thinks she runs the world. Let me tell you, she might have rich parents, but that doesn't mean she's a class act. You should have seen her. Completely hammered after being here for less than half an hour. It was disgusting."

"And there were some groomsmen here, too, weren't there?"

The hostess's eyebrows furrowed. "How do you know that?"

"Thanks," Peter said. He turned on his heel.

Jessica followed quickly after him as he hurried back outside. "What is it? You figured something out, didn't you?"

"I have. But we have to move fast."

"We haven't found Kaia yet!"

"She wasn't the one who pushed Cory." Peter's heart hammered in his chest. "We don't have time—we have to stop the wedding."

CHAPTER
ELEVEN
STILL LAKE RESORT

"WHAT IS GOING ON?" Jessica asked, keeping her voice low as she and Peter hurried into the resort. He'd been so focused on the drive back that she hadn't dared ask for fear of breaking his concentration. "Do you know who pushed him?"

"I think I've got it figured out. I need just a little more. We need to find Arista."

"Arista?" Jessica thought about how she had been sobbing earlier in the day and how she and her parents were pushing hard for the wedding to continue. Her skin crawled—was her baby brother about to marry an attempted murderer? She clenched her fists as she guided Peter to the elevator. "I know which room she's in. Let's go."

Her toes tapped against the floor impatiently as the elevator made its way to the fourth floor. As soon as the doors dinged open, Jessica seized Peter's hand and pulled him down the hallway. They had less than forty-five minutes until the wedding. She wasn't about to let her brother marry some black widow! Possibilities rushed through her mind about what could happen if he did.

She knocked hard on Arista's door as soon as they arrived, panting with how quickly she'd run down the hallway. There were sounds of laughter on the other side, but they seemed subdued. She knocked louder.

Moments later, an angry-looking bridesmaid yanked the door open. "What? We're trying to get ready here."

"I need to talk to Arista," Jessica said.

"Why?"

She thought quickly. "I have a necklace my mother gave me when I married. I thought it would bring Arista and Michael luck if she would wear it down the aisle, or maybe she could have it as part of the bouquet or in her pocket. Just... I want to welcome her into the family."

Jessica smiled at the bridesmaid, whose angry expression softened.

The bridesmaid leaned against the doorframe. "Oh. That's sweet. Arista is getting ready with her mother down the hall. Room 426."

"Thanks."

Jessica turned on her heel. She brought her breathing under control again as she and Peter went to room 426. She inhaled deeply and put on a false smile as she knocked at the door.

The door opened to Arista's mother. Her expression was stiff as she looked Jessica up and down. "You aren't wearing that to the wedding, are you?"

"I'd like to talk to Arista, please," Jessica replied coolly. "I have something to give her."

"Arista is getting ready for her marriage."

A small voice spoke from behind her. "It's all right, Mother. I'd like to talk to Jessica."

She came to the doorway. Her dress was beautiful, with a creamy tone that complimented her dark hair. Her eyes were red from crying, though, which couldn't be hidden even with the contour makeup and perfectly curled hair.

Peter shut the door behind them as they entered.

When Arista saw him, her expression dropped. "You're that cop Jessica is dating, aren't you?"

"I'm not," Peter said.

Jessica felt a ridiculous surge of disappointment. She knew they weren't dating. They were friends. Good friends.

Peter continued. "I'm a lawyer. And you're going to need one. So, tell me... why did you try to kill Cory Atkins?"

CHAPTER
TWELVE
ROOM 426

ARISTA SANK INTO A NEARBY CHAIR, covering her face with her hands. Her mother harrumphed as she put an arm around her daughter.

"See here! You have no right to waltz in here and accuse my baby girl of something like that! What is wrong with you?" The mother trembled with rage as she glared first at Peter and then Jessica. "I should have known your family would be riff-raff but to sabotage your own brother's chances at happiness?"

She was very good at turning the situation back on them; Peter had to admit. But he had spent too much time in the courtroom to let such an obvious tactic phase him.

"On the contrary, I'm trying to help. You see, I have a pretty good idea of what happened already; I just need to fill in a few of the holes before I take this to Detective Cray." Peter was sure to keep his voice gentle. All the clues he had found pointed to more than what was obvious. "You said that they were all getting drunk last night, yes?"

Jessica nodded, a puzzled expression on her face.

"And when they returned to the hotel, Arista was so wasted she couldn't get to her room on her own." Peter folded his arms. "They weren't just drunk. They were high as well. Cory told you about

Roundhouse, didn't he? And when you went there with your party, he was waiting."

Arista started to cry. Her mother looked lost, opening and closing her mouth quickly. She made a strangled noise as she stepped toward the door, but Arista reached out and grabbed her hand.

"I'm going to get your father," Arista's mother said.

"I want you to stay," Arista rasped. Tears flooded down her face. "You're right. We went to Roundhouse. I was just looking to have fun. I've never done drugs, and when Cory offered me some last night, I didn't want to take any. I was already drunk enough, so I ordered mocktails. But…"

"But he slipped something in your drink. And since you were already drunk, your bridesmaids didn't notice." Peter felt the anger rising in him. If anyone had tried to do this to his daughter, he'd have killed them.

Arista chewed her lip. "I don't know. I didn't feel any different. It occurred to me that I should sober up. But I just seemed to lose more and more. I lost all my inhibitions when the groomsmen started making out with the bridesmaids…."

Jessica knelt beside her chair. "Cory pressed you to make out with him."

"He drugged her," Arista's mother snapped.

"I never was attracted to Cory. I thought he was kind of weird and socially inept, but I felt sorry for him since he never had any luck with girlfriends. He said that we should just have a friendly kiss. I agreed, but then he grabbed and shoved me into the wall." Arista closed her eyes.

Jessica grasped her hand as Peter moved a little closer, wanting to offer comfort.

"It's not your fault," Arista's mother said. "Honey, if Michael really is the man you think he is, he wouldn't care."

"Mother, just stop!" Arista jerked away from her mother, squeezing Jessica's hand tighter. "I'm so tired of your snide comments toward Michael. You've been pushing and pushing for this wedding not to be canceled despite everything. You're the one who told me not to tell him—I'm wondering why!"

Arista's mother huffed, and Peter moved to the side, blocking her path to the door. He kept his eyes on Arista, though. "So, Cory assaulted you."

"He didn't… he only kissed me," Arista protested.

Peter sighed. "Legally and morally, it's still assault."

"Well… that's all that happened. He pushed me against the wall and kissed me. One of the servers jumped in and pushed him off me. She started shouting at him, saying that he promised her Michael would want her back or something. I don't remember. She made us leave."

"And on the way back to the hotel, Cory sent you a picture of the kiss and told you to meet him at the lake," Peter continued.

Arista flinched. "How could you know that?"

"When I talked to Kaia—one of Michael's ex-girlfriends—she mentioned Cory turning Michael against her, and since Michael and Cory bonded in the first place because of a breakup, including Cory being cheated on, I realized he pushed that same narrative on his best friend." Peter shook his head in disgust. "Michael told Jessica that Cory knew how to have fun, but he wasn't engaged in the party. He wanted to stay sober for a reason."

"He told me to meet him at the lake," Arista whispered. "He said he'd show Michael the pictures and tell him I tried to seduce him. He said he wanted money, but… But I didn't go! I planned on telling Michael, but I passed out as soon as I got to my room."

"I know. Jessica told me she helped you to your room because you could hardly walk. You weren't in any state to attack Cory." He finally turned his gaze from Arista to her mother, his expression still calm and emotionless. "She wasn't, but what parent, upon learning that their child was drugged and being blackmailed, wouldn't want vengeance?"

Arista's mother stared coldly at him.

"Mother?" Arista's voice rose in pitch. "What… no. You didn't know."

"Except she did," Peter said, creeping forward. "You were looking for reasons to break them up because you didn't think Michael was good enough. Was it someone you hired to follow Arista, or did you plant spyware on her phone?"

Arista's mother shook her head. "I don't know what you're talking about."

"Detective Cray said what happened to Cory was an accident, that he found the bloody rock Cory must have hit his head on. But I found Cory face-down. The scene showed signs of a struggle, and the detective was too sharp to ignore evidence like the broken heel we found. There's no reason he shouldn't have found it, either."

"You're insane." Arista's mother fluttered, her head swiveling as though searching for an escape.

Peter continued to advance. He would have a lot of sympathy for this woman and her husband, except for one thing. "There's only one reason Cray would ignore the broken heel we found in the lake because he planted it. You planned first to pin the attack on Kaia, didn't you?"

"I didn't—"

"You paid Cory to convince Kaia to try and seduce Michael, so you could have a reason to break up the marriage. When that didn't work, you realized if you could get the detective to interrupt the wedding and accuse Michael of murder... well, that was even better."

Arista sagged against Jessica, her eyes wide with betrayal. "Mother?"

"I... I... he's not right for you!" the mother exploded. Then she slapped both hands to her mouth.

Peter let out a heavy breath. So, the truth was out. He pulled his phone from his pocket. Time to call his contact in the FBI, Tiff. She'd ensure a proper investigation was done—into Arista's parents and the corrupt Detective Cray.

EPILOGUE
THE CESSNA

"SO, when Kaia said she knew what happened, she was referring to Cory drugging Arista," Jessica said.

It had been a very intense, confusing last few hours on their so-called vacation, and she was more than ready to return to life's daily chaos. She was bundled up in a fuzzy blanket as Peter drove back toward Pine Grove through clear skies.

"Yeah," Peter agreed. "Though I don't know if she planned to tell Michael or not. I think she thought she still had a chance with him still... and apparently, she cheated on him with several men before Cory met her at a party. She didn't know he and Michael were friends but...."

Jessica shook her head. Her brother certainly had a dramatic love life. "I'm just glad he and Arista have agreed to go to couple's counseling about this and not rush into getting married."

Peter nodded once. "It's a good call. And I'm glad that Cory is going to recover. He deserves the trial that's coming to him."

Jessica nodded in agreement.

The unfortunate thing about this was that she never got to ask Peter where he was in their relationship. Now it just seemed a little silly. She sighed heavily, resting her head against the window.

"Penny for your thoughts?" Peter asked.

"I just… don't know why love has to be so hard."

Peter was silent for a moment and then murmured, "It doesn't have to be."

"It doesn't? Look at what happened at this wedding. Isn't this what happened to you and Melanie? To Henry and me? Love is hard. Sometimes, it's too hard."

"I disagree. Love is simple. The hard part is life. Really knowing each other, staying in love even when you see the other person's faults." Peter hummed as he watched the clouds pensively. "If two people know what they want, and they know themselves, then it's easier. They can be open and honest with what they want."

Jessica's heart skipped a beat. "Well… what if I know what I want?"

Peter smiled at her, his eyes sparkling. "Then tell me."

*

TIMMS RESIDENCE

Marconi dumped the hanger overalls in the corner of his room and gently nudged a cat out of his way. That had been a far more dramatic trip than he'd intended. Peter had figured out the mystery himself on the plus side, and Marconi hadn't had to reveal his presence. He was still impressed with the swing that old woman took when she brained the guy on the docks.

If he hadn't been watching to pull the man out of the water, Peter would have investigated a murder.

Aunt Verna hummed as she entered the room, carrying the giant sandwich Marconi had just told her he wasn't hungry for. "Are you taking care of yourself and staying out of trouble?"

Marconi sighed as he took the sandwich. Better to capitulate. "I am. And I'm keeping Peter out of trouble, too."

Aunt Verna smiled and patted the top of his head. "Good boy. Make sure you keep it that way."

The End
Did you enjoy *Pine Grove Mysteries*?

Please consider rating it on Goodreads, Bookbub, or your favorite retailer. Reviews help me reach new readers.

Read *Pine Grove Mysteries Volume 2* for the next 5 stories!

Join my Newsletter for updates and giveaways!
www.daisylandishromance.com

ABOUT THE AUTHOR

Daisy Landish is a romance and cozy mystery author living whose clean and sweet novellas have tugged at readers' heartstrings around the world. When she's not writing love stories, Daisy spends her time reading, hiking at dawn, and riding into the sunset on her horse, Rosebud.

www.daisylandishromance.com

facebook.com/daisylandishromance
x.com/daisy_landish
instagram.com/daisylandishbooks
amazon.com/author/daisylandish
bookbub.com/authors/daisy-landish
goodreads.com/Daisy_Landish

ALSO BY DAISY LANDISH

Clean Regency Romance

The Lady Series - The Allington Collection

The Lady Series - The Gillingham Collection

The Lady Series - The Blackmore Collection

The Lady Series - The Norrington Collection

Clean Contemporary Romance

Maplewood Grove Series

Love on Spruce Island

Second Chance

Cherry Tree Island

The Wedding Trio

Extra Credit

Counting on the Cowboy

Focusing on the Cowboy

Mistletoe Magic

Grounded at Christmas

Cozy Mysteries

Sophie Brooks Mysteries

Jane and Kennedy Daniels Mysteries

Pine Grove Mysteries

Annie Archer Paranormal Mysteries

Wilma Wade Holiday Mysteries

Mike and Maddie Mysteries

Mystic Moonhaven Mysteries

Sweater Weather: Cozy Mysteries for Fall

Summer Vibes: Cozy Mysteries for Summer